Samuel McClurg Osmond

**Sulamith**

A Metrical Romance

Samuel McClurg Osmond

**Sulamith**
*A Metrical Romance*

ISBN/EAN: 9783337347796

Printed in Europe, USA, Canada, Australia, Japan

Cover: Foto ©Andreas Hilbeck / pixelio.de

More available books at **www.hansebooks.com**

# A METRICAL ROMANCE.

BY

SAMUEL McCLURG OSMOND, D.D.

PHILADELPHIA:

THE JAS. B. RODGERS PRINTING COMPANY,

52 AND 54 NORTH SIXTH ST.

1892.

HONEY sweetness drops from thy lips,
    My sister-bride !
    Honey and milk are on thy tongue,
The smell of thy robes is like that of Lebanon.
A garden enclosed is my sister-bride,
A fencèd well, a sealed-up spring.

                    —*Song of Songs.*

# CONTENTS.

•

# PROEM.

 HAD been musing on that mystic song
  Of love and longing, which—as some have
  deemed—
Is in the sacred canon strangely found :
"Strangely," say they, "because so much attuned
To key-notes given forth by human hearts
When but an earth-born passion sweeps their chords."

But well I knew that its melodious strains,
So soft and low with yearning tenderness,
Or tremulous with thrills of passionate pain,
Or jubilant with a triumphal joy,
Were all as angels' wings to saintly souls,
On which they soared to heavenly ecstacies
And purest raptures of the love divine.

Yet even to me had doubt unbidden come,
That he who wove into his crown of crowns

This brightest of its gems, the Song of Songs,
Had, when he set its peerless splendors there,
Of aught else dreamed than common hopes and fears,
The bliss and anguish, trust and faithfulness,
And fond communings of two kindred hearts
Together drawn, through all that interposed,
By interweaving ties that make them one.

Nor seemed such theme unworthy to employ
The wisdom of the wisest of mankind,
Or to invoke the inspiring breath of Him
Who made man male and female, each for each,
Crowning the bliss of Eden with their love,
Ordaining wedlock as the fount of life
And joy and weal for all humanity.

Then came to me the thought of Eden's loss,
And sadder loss of Eden-innocence;
And how, in ever-deepening guilt and shame,
The apostate race of man had drifted far
From its divine ideals, and not least
From that of wedded love's sweet sanctity;
And how the very best and holiest,
As faithful Abraham and Israel,
And David, who was after God's own heart,

Had cast into the shadowed springs of Home,
Which God had meant should keep the world's life pure,
The curse and poison of polygamy.

Much did I marvel that from Solomon,
Who went this downward way his father trod
Until, at last, he reached its yawning depths,
And who so prostituted womanhood
To basest uses, that her virtues fled
Abashed, and left her such sole dower of shame—
Of shame and falsehood, that in all the thousand
He knew too well, he found not one above
What he had made her—not one pure and true!—
Great was my wonder, that from such a source
Should flow this limpid stream of sacred song,
So tuneful with the sweetness of a love
Artless as Nature's self, fresh, virginal,
Commixt of mind and heart, of soul and sense,
Yet free from taint of evil consciousness .
As that of the first pair who, hand in hand,
Roved through the flowery haunts of Paradise,
Clothed with but innocence, untaught of shame.

Was he whose life so desecrated love,
Who dragged it from its throne of purity,
Sullied and slain, the one who also sang

Love's sweetest praises? Was the cunning hand
Which wrought it deadly wrong the hand that painted,
In colors vivid as the rainbow's hues,
Its unstained beauty? Did the very lips,
That on it breathed the blight of their pollution,
Give utterance to thoughts and images
Which even Inspiration could employ,
In setting forth that holy mystery,
The love of Christ and of His church blood-bought,
The Lamb and the Lamb's Bride, forever one?

So queried I, in sore perplexity,
Until my mind, with fruitless musing wearied,
Drifted in dreams. Then Fancy plied her oars,
But Reason kept her hold upon the helm.

# SULAMITH.

— • —

## I.

### AMMINADIB.

**A** TIDAL flood of fierce and bloody fight
Had rolled its surges, ere the close of day,
Over the summit of a Syrian hill ;
And now upon its trampled, gory sod,
Or underneath its tangled vines—their leaves
Drenched and still dripping with the crimson spray—
Were strewn the wrecks, the dying and the dead.

The host of Israel had chased the foe
Down to the valley, and had scattered him,
Even as chaff of summer threshing floor
Is swept upon the whirlwind.

As the shades
Of evening deepened, to the vantage ground,
Crowded with Syria's deserted tents,
The victors hastened back to seize the spoils
Won by their valor, or to find what thirst,
Hunger and weariness more keenly crave,
When long deferred—refreshment and repose.

Foremost of the returning host, had sped
The gleaming chariot of Amminadib,
Its coursers, famed for fleetness, flecked with foam
From unslacked driving up the steep hillside.
No pause it made amid the scattered spoil,
Or for the food or couch of sheltering tent;
But onward drove until the charioteer
Drew sudden rein before the ghastly swaths
Of bloody forms, mown by the scythe of war
Through serried ranks of Israel's enemies.

Oh, not to feast his eyes upon these piles
Of slaughtered foemen did Amminadib,
From his stayed chariot, look upon that scene
Of untold horrors—doubly such to him,
As first he saw them in the spectral light

Of the weird moonrise.   True, of Judah's chiefs
None loved the storm of battle more than he,
Or found in its stern havoc fiercer joy ;
Yet his heroic heart was pitiful
And tender as a woman's.   When the shock
And stress of strife had ceased, oft came to him
A strange relenting, a resistless tide
Of passionate feeling, that would bear him on,
Until as now he stood and gazed upon
The very sights at which his soul recoiled—
The stony faces, the reproaching eyes
Of those on whom perchance his reeking blade
Had dealt the deadly strokes which laid them low.

He knew that, in such conflict as had raged
Upon the hill top, few had been the strokes
Which had not reached their aim, a foeman's
      heart ;
And that, through Joab's matchless discipline,
Nor less, through the warm brotherhood that bound
The hearts of Israel's warriors each to each,
Not one of these, if wounded, would be left
Unsuccored on the field where Israel's arms
Had put the foe to flight.

And still his eye
Scans all the field, with scrutiny as keen
As if some living friend or kinsman dear
Might be discerned among its crowded dead,
In mortal peril or in helpless pain.

But neither moan nor motion told of life,
Nor aught beside, save but the hurried tramp
And flaring torches of a chosen band,
Who, at his word, had followed as they could,
Prepared to give the aid that might be needed
In furtherance of his merciful intent.
These hear his brief commands, then sally forth,
With food and water furnished, to make search
So thorough for all faint or wounded ones,
That when Amminadib, that night, should seek
Rest for his wearied frame and burdened heart,
No haunting thought of hunger or of thirst
Or anguish unrelieved that might have been,
Should with accusing visions vex his sleep.

Awhile he waited in his chariot;
But briefly, for his stirred and restless heart
Rebelled against inaction.  He had spied

An unobstructed way, on either side
Lined with the slain, with breadth enough between
For easy passage of the chariot wheels ;
Along this route they leisurely proceed ;
Oft pausing while Amminadib, alert,
Makes eager scrutiny of all in sight ;
But fruitlessly, until at length they come
To where the roadway narrows. There, in front
Of the uprearing steeds, a manly form,
Richly appareled—his sword sheath embossed
With jewels glittering in the brightening beams
Of the full, cloudless moon—half gains his feet ;
Then prostrate falls, as if from failing strength,
That serves him not for flight, or from despair
That urges acquiescence in the death
Which chariot wheels or hoofs of plunging horses
Might sooner bring than slowly bleeding wounds,
That, drop by drop, would drain his life-springs dry.

But scarce had sunk the fainting Syrian
Back to the grassy sod steeped in his blood,
Before Amminadib was by his side.
He sprinkled water on his clammy brow,
And pressed a flagon to his parchèd lips,

On which they closed instinctively, and quaffed
Of its reviving cordial eager draughts,
That fed anew the flickering flame of life,
Until, with upraised head and searching eyes,
He gazed, as if he fain would read the soul
Of him who bent above him.   First there swept
Over his pallid, noble countenance
An early dawn of wonder, cold and keen ;
And then faint kindlings of a new-born hope ;
Nor long delayed to brighten and to glow
The sunrise flush of confidence and joy.

Amminadib would fain have called for help,
To bear the wounded warrior to a place
Where fitting care and shelter might be found,
But that, with air of firmly fixed resolve,
He plainly showed that he would not be moved
From his poor resting-place.   Then courteously,
With deep, clear tones and still unfaded light
Of glad expectancy upon his face,
His thankfulness expressed, and his surprise
At kindness rendered by a foeman's hand ;
And further thus he spake :

"Oh, Israelite,
And Chief among thy people, hear my words—
The last these lips of mine shall ever breathe
To mortal listener : In yonder village,
That sleeps within the shadow of the hill,
Unwalled and undefended, are the homes
Of those who still are left to own me lord.
For all its males of strength to carry arms
Lie here around me ; since not one of them
Was molded of the common stuff that makes
Swift fugitives from danger and from death,
In the lost battle. Here they fought and fell.

"Rising above the humbler cottages
That cluster round it, like a parent pine
Above the kindred trees of later growth
Sprung from its scattered seed, behold the home
That late was mine, where, wholly unaware
Of evil, dreaded long, impending now,
My faithful, loving spouse, for my return,
With busy hands, prepares home's brightest cheer,—
Only alas ! for those who soon shall come
To bring it desolation and despair.

2

"Four children, by the favor of the gods,
Were given us, and there remain of these
Three ruddy boys, who show their warrior blood :
But one, a gentle daughter, is no more.

"Oh, stranger, enemy, who yet hast shown
Such kindness in my dire extremity ;
And in whose looks the heart-depths I can see,
Whence gush the living waters that have brought
Refreshment to my thirsting, fainting soul ;—
Forgive me that I plead for further grace,
And pray, with dying breath, that thou wilt swear
By dread Jehovah, whom thou worshipest,
And who, at last, I learn, from what I see
And feel, is mightier far than Rimmon,
The god of Syria who, on Syrian soil,
Sees Syrians shamed before their enemies ;—
Yes, by Jehovah, called the Merciful,
(And rightly so full well this day I know,
Even by the mercy thou His worshiper
Hast shown to one who is thy nation's foe.)
By Him who seems the God of Heaven and Earth,
Swear that my widowed wife and little ones
Shall fall into no other hands than thine,—

Shall be thy captives or whate'er thou wilt.
Take first this ring with priceless rubies set,
And this good sword that never yet was stained
With aught save foeman's blood in battle shed,—
Nay, nay, refuse me not this last request ;
Nor leave them to be seized by other hands ;
But let them be to thee, in coming years,
The witnesses of this thy oath to me,
That thou wilt truly, kindly deal with them
Concerning whom I charge thee, as thou wouldst
Thy God shall deal with thee."

                    Amminadib
Raised his right hand toward Heaven, and with
    bared brow,
In deepest reverence, sware by Him who made
The heavens and the earth, that faithfully,
So far as in him lay, he would fulfill
The sacred charge committed to his hands.
Ere yet his words were spoken, o'er the moon
A veil of fleecy, silvered cloud was spread,
And when he stooped and closely looked again
Upon the Syrian's face, a darker cloud
Had cast upon its pale unchanging features
The deep, chill shadow of Death's mystery.

## II.

## CAPTIVE AND CAPTOR.

WIFT years had sped since o'er the Syrian hill
The blood-red surges of fierce battle rolled,
And left the Syrian chief a stranded wreck.
The kindness shown him by Amminadib,
And greater pledged and wrought for those he loved,
Had been as bread upon the waters cast,
As seed which, though for others only sown,
Had also yielded the unselfish sower
Such fruitage as he had not dared to dream
Could bless and beautify his barren life:
For all its tender leaves and dewy blossoms
Had shriveled in the blaze of its hot noon.
True, golden gains had come to him, but ever
With losses that impoverished his heart,
And left it vainly hungering for love.
Within the compass of one fleeting year,

Which with a wedding feast had been begun,
A husband and a father he had been,
Then wifeless, childless—hopeless, but for God.

Rays of the sunset, golden arrows piercing
The crystal showers that pour from drifting clouds,
Bear most aloft the bow with promise fraught;
So, when his tears fell on the graves of these
Last, dearest of his dead, that light which shines
Brightest as sets the sun of earth-born hope,
With more than iridescent beauty clothed,
For his sad soul, exalted thoughts of Heaven;
And all the glories of the world grew dim.
Then noblest aims and purposes of life
Unsprung from out the stormy depths of woe.
He would no longer live for love or pleasure,
But for his God, his country and his king;
And on the vacant throne which happiness
Before had filled, a rose-crowned, smiling queen,
Stern Faithfulness should wield imperiously
His sceptre, partly iron, partly gold.

Harsh schooling of his native gentleness
Had left his tender, pitying heart unspoiled,

And, by authority which had been given,
Though grudgingly, by Joab, he had saved
The Syrian captives from atrocities
To ancient warfare common ; most of all,
Had shown the chieftain's family and town,
Such thoughtful kindness as had greatly moved
The wonder of the lady now their head.
As yet she knew not that her lord was slain,
And fondly hoping for his prompt return,
Would not be rescued from the coming storm
Of pillage and destruction, but postponed.
Therefore, Amminadib reluctantly—
Well knowing, that in the engulfing waves
Of great calamity are swallowed up
All secondary cares and interests,
And that one stunning blow of trouble dulls
The sense to lighter strokes,—thus reasoning,
Had laid upon her hands, outstretched at last,
The sword and ring.  To her quick intuition,
These were undoubted tokens of the truth
That rendered her benumbed and bleeding heart
Indifferent to all the world beside.
Her captors now might work their will upon her.
Her children caught her acquiescent mood,

And she and they were borne, by such conveyance
As could be furnished, to Jerusalem,
And to Amminadib's own spacious home
Which long had been a sole, sad dwelling-place
For bitter memories of buried joys.

The foes of David, for the time, were crushed;
And Israel's surviving warriors,
Sore spent with hardship, toil and battle-strain,
Had learned—what else they never could have
    known—
How sweet are home and rest!

Amminadib—
In this unlike his fellows—sadly knew,
Familiar scenes could yield him no repose.
To look upon them would but stir afresh
The fountains of his sorrow and unrest.

The king had given him, for use and profit,
A wide uncultured tract of glebe and forest,
Rugged, but fertile, 'mid the lonely wilds
And rocky steeps of Lebanon. To this
His thoughts had turned, and soon his chariot

Had borne him thither. But, at his departure,
He gave his Syrian wards, with strictest charges,
Into the hands of his devoted servants.
Of these, one trusted, honored most, named Agar,
An Israelitish woman, gentle, strong,
Devout, and zealous for her faith and nation,
Had been his mother's handmaid, and, when he
Was left in early childhood motherless,
Had scarcely less to him than mother proved.
She knew and well performed her master's wishes :
The lights of the old home shone out again,
Its hearthstone, cold so long, now brightly blazed
With genial welcome, as for cherished guests ;
And all that gold could buy or thought could plan
Was lavished on the widow and her sons.

Soon rang the walls with unaccustomed sounds
Of boyish laughter, for the heart of childhood
Is from its sorrows easily beguiled.
But she, whose griefs the anxious servitor
So sedulously sought to charm away,
Was unresponsive. Not a smile or word
Showed slightest heed to those who were around her ;
Barely some faintest motherly regard—

From instinct more than reason—for her sons.
Month after month she wore upon her face
The changeless look of one transformed to stone,
As all the joys of life had vanished from her;
Rather as if it were but sculptured grief,
And pain and hopelessness together wrought
Upon a face of marble, pale and cold,—
A fascination to the gazer's eye,
And yet a terror to his shrinking heart,
Lest haply it should haunt his nightly dreams,
And grow to be a weariness forever.

Agar had learned, from hard and painful lessons
Of by-gone years, that for such hopeless grief
God's peace and mercy only furnish cure.
But she, for whose soul's life she travailed sore,
Knew only of the gods of wood and stone,
Of gold, and brass, and iron, deaf and blind,
And powerless to pity or to save.
At length, with wisdom greater than her state,
Born of her yearning love and sympathy,
She gained by indirection what she sought:
She clothed in simplest words the Hebrew tales,
Which have, through all the ages, proved a charm

For childhood's heart, and told them o'er and o'er—
The mother near—to the rapt Syrian boys:
Of blameless Joseph by his brethren sold,
And how God turned their evil into good;
Of infant Moses from fierce Pharaoh saved,
To lead, in after years, his people forth
From iron bondage to the promised land;
Of Ruth, the Moabitess, who had come,
Widowed and poor, but dowered with loveliness,
To trust beneath Jehovah's sheltering wing.
Or, with low, lulling tones, such as might soothe
A restless child to sleep, she sung or chanted
The songs of Zion, plaintive oft with griefs,
Yet ever fraught with sacred hopes and longings,
That wafted troubled souls upon their wings
Up to the heavenly hills whence cometh help.

　　　She, for whose sake, with many a burdened
　　　　　prayer,
This artful artlessness was chiefly wrought,
At length grew heedful.　Then there came a time—
The first since fell the blow that fateful night—
When her tears started and soon fell like rain.
The light had reached their fountain, and the warmth

Melted her frozen heart; and after that
She talked with Agar; but of one theme only—
The greatest—God! And Agar's glowing speech
Was as of one inspired. And so the night
That knew no stars now broke and rolled away,
With all its hideous dreams of Baal and Molech,
And Ashteroth and Rimmon, lust and blood,
And utter dreadful void of hope or healing
For bleeding hearts. Thus Agar's work was wrought.

She, in whose soul the quenchless light had
    dawned,
And scattered superstition's direful night,
Long seemed like one who, in deep poverty,
Has found a treasure that is boundless wealth,
And o'er it bends with such absorbing joy,
Or guards it with such unremitting care,
That all things else, however great or dear,
Are meanwhile little heeded. New-found peace
Took full possession of her mind and heart,
And all their elevated faculties
Found sole employment in the higher range
To which she had been borne, by a transition
Swift and bewildering, as when happy spirits,

Loosed from their fleshly bonds, entranced and
    thrilled
With Heaven's transcendent glories, grow forgetful
Of earthly scenes and friends the best beloved.


    But, with the healing wrought upon her soul,
A kindred salutary influence
Brought back the brightness to her eye, the bloom
To her paled cheek; and then, from less to more,
Something of natural interest and feeling
Evinced their presence by a questioning look,
Which grew to be so wistfully intense,
That Agar noticed it and made reply.
She told her of their master and his home,
And of his far-famed steeds and chariots,
His valor, piety and gentleness.
But as the stream of loving eulogy
Kept flowing, still, upon the listener's face
Deepened the shadow of perplexity,
To which, at last, her lips gave utterance.
"Oh, why," she cried, "am I, and these, my sons
Thus treated in the home of Syria's foe;
Its comforts, its abundance, even its love
Upon us lavished, as if all were ours?"

Agar made answer that Amminadib,
Who brought them thither from the Syrian war,
Had so commanded.  Then, as not before,
Flashed on the questioner's mind the certainty,
That this Amminadib, whose glowing praises
Agar had spoken, of whose generous bounty
She and her children were the living proofs,
Was he who had in battle slain her lord,
And made her children orphans.  Had he not—
Though why, she vainly queried—brought to her
The ring and sword, that none could e'er have taken,
Save from his lifeless hands?  Oh, bitter thought,
That she and hers must eat his bread!  Her lips
Were sealed upon her anguish, but her soul
Cried out to her new Helper night and day.
She would have fled, but that a sense of honor
Kept her from throwing off the only bond
That held her to her state—her captor's kindness.
Agar was quick to note her deep distress,
But could not learn its cause or give relief;
Hence sent swift summons to Amminadib,
To which his presence speedy answer gave.

More than the urgency of Agar's message,

The lash of self-reproach had served to quicken
His homeward journey : for, in the absorption
Of other interests, his Syrian wards
Had been well nigh forgotten ; and too long,
He now could realize, had been postponed
The full recital he had meant to give
The widowed one of how her husband died,
And of the last fond wishes. he had spoken.
Thus had he left her wounded heart to ache
With dark and torturing uncertainties,
From which, at least, she might have been relieved
By his disclosures.   Scarcely taking time
For Agar's narrative—that gave him comfort,
Yet roused his apprehensions—he straightway
Sought her apartments, and soon gazed upon
Her now unveiléd but averted face ;
And, without needless ceremony, poured
His story into her attentive ears.
It gave reality and vividness
To what had been a vague and shadowy grief,
And hence, as never hitherto, the fountains
Of her great deep of woe were broken up.
But when the tumult of their overflow
At length abated, to her thought there came

Some dawning sense of the rare nobleness
Of him who stood before her, and her heart
Reproached her keenly for the causeless wrong,
That, in her blinded rashness, she had done
To one who, next to God Himself, deserved
Her gratitude and honor.  Then her eyes,
Still with their tears suffused, were raised to his,
Wet also with the manly drops that fell
For pity of her woe and helplessness ;
And, at that moment, in the soul of each
Was born a feeling which, through months that
    followed
While they were still apart, grew into strength ;
But never otherwise than side by side
With loyal, tender, undimmed memories
Of those who but in memory now were theirs.

Again the chariot of Amminadib,
More swift than ever, flashed along the road
That leads from Lebanon to Jerusalem.
He came to claim a warrior's legal right,
As plainly written in the code of Moses,
To wed the female captive he has taken ;
Yet, as if she, not he, had been the captor,

He humbly sued her to become his wife,
And, to her yielding heart, sued not in vain.


The Syrian vine, whose roots had deeply struck
Into the richness of Judean soil,
Was not unfruitful ; and the olive plants
In beauty grew, around the well-filled board
Spread for Amminadib :—but spread no more
In presence of his enemies.  Hot words,
Which he had spoken of the cruelties
Practised by Joab on his vanquished foes,
Had made a widening breach between the two.
King David loved and prized Amminadib,
And as the only way in which to shield him
From Joab's seldom less than fatal wrath,
Had, with all honor, given him discharge
From warfare.  Then, for his abandoned sword,
He plied the plowshare ; for the warrior's spear,
The pruning hook, with which he ere long won
Bloodless and blameless victories, that turned
The wilderness into a fruitful field,
And wreathed the mountain slopes of Lebanon
With blossoming vines and orchards.  So had flown
Swift years of love and peace on downy wings.

## III.

## LEBANON.

UPON a rock that rose precipitous,
  A jutting buttress on the mountain side,
  Rounded and fluted by the elements,
With flattened top that formed its ample platform,
Was reared the cottage of Amminadib.
There, amid Lebanon's cool and breezy heights,
He and his household, yearly, refuge found
From torrid heats that all the summer long
Drank up the strength of those who on the plains
Or in the cities had their dwelling place.
The mountain was its safeguard from the rear;
In front the scaleless rock a fortress stood,
Impregnable to every human foe.
A winding roadway to the fastness led,
So narrow it could easily be made
Impassable for all who came unwelcomed.

3

A streamlet, leaping from the mountain top,
Cold with the snows that melted at its source,
Out of the rock, near to the cottage door,
Had scooped a round, deep basin, whence it welled
With overflowing fulness, and was led,
By artificial channels, wheresoe'er
It best might serve the ends of use and beauty,
Then found its way adown the rock's deep grooves,
In countless trickling rivulets, that brought
Moisture and greenness to the slope below.
Oh, never was a home of earth environed
With greater wealth of grandeur or of beauty :—
The background filled with mountain ruggedness,
But on the foreground smooth declivities,
The terraced vineyards and the scattered groups
Of pine and palm, the oak and terebinth,
The fig and olive, and the flocks and herds
That grazed on stretches of green pasturage,
Which coalesced and widened to the plain
Laced with the flashing sheen of silvery streams,
And by far mountains dimly limited.

Well might the inmates of such favored home
More than sufficient for each other prove,

And little heed a far-off world's ambitions,
Its vain disquietudes and hollow joys.
Their souls upon its feasts of beauty throve,
Nor failed to drink of beauty's living Spring.
With healthful food their bodies were sustained,
And vitalized with purest mountain air;
Hence both grew strong for life's supremest duties
And those that to its lowlier sphere pertained.
The Syrian boys, to youthful manhood grown,
Some roughness in their brawn and vigor showed;
But they were sound of heart, and well repaid
The care which to their training had been given;
And staunchest aid their hands had lent in bringing
Order and fruitfulness from out the chaos
Of brambles, thickets, rocks and barrenness.
Thus on themselves was marked improvement
    wrought;
For labor oft as much of culture gives
To them who labor as to that on which
The work is worthily done. The younger children,
Though never stinted in their happy play-time,
Had, too, their little tasks—scarce more than sport—
But which yet served the lesson to impress,
That life is not to be all holiday.

Of these, first born, the maiden Sulamith,
Though much her mother's helper and companion
In household cares and duties, with her brothers,
Oft scaled the mountain steeps in bold adventure,
Or helped to tend the orchards and the vines;
Trimmed their luxuriant growth, or, with deft hands,
Plucked the ripe, purple clusters for the wine-press,
Or gaily gleaned after the merry reapers,
Even as the fair ancestress of King David,
More toilfully and with a soberer mien,
Once gleaned the harvest field of Bethlehem,
And charmed the heart of its benignant owner.

Closer than filial and paternal bond,
Did common tastes and kindred sympathies
Together draw the daughter and her sire;
And beautiful it was to see the joy
They had in one another. Side by side,
Amminadib's fleet chariot bore them past
Historic scenes with thrilling memories fraught.
Of these they spoke until their souls were fired
With patriotic zeal, or upward borne,
On wings of grateful praise to Him whose power
Had saved His people from their enemies.

Her eager questions drew, from hidden depths,
The stores of wisdom which his life had garnered.
He taught her of the Law, and how its spirit
More sacred than its letter should be held,—
A germ of deathless life in fruitful souls,
E'en when the withered husk should fall away;
And that no services or sacrifice
Gave God delight apart from love and mercy,
Or broken heart that sorrowed for its sin.
And oft he made to live and move before her—
Illumined by his vivid glowing praises—
The noblest types of true, pure womanhood;
And poured the torrents of his fierce invective
On those who lightly held that, which to woman
Above her life should evermore be prized.
Of Israel's glorious hope and destiny
They also spoke, and longed for clearer sight
Of that glad, promised day when, over her
And all the nations, David's Son and Lord,
The Prince of peace, should reign in righteousness.
And much their converse was of Israel's past,
Her sons and daughters of heroic mold,—
Moses and Joshua, Gideon and Samson;
And him who all beside excelled in greatness,

Who, when a stripling, slew the boasting giant,
And, from the bleating flocks he shepherded,
Through thronging obstacles, had made his way
To Israel's throne, by him now lifted high
Above earth's loftiest; Zeruiah's sons,
And other mightier, since of nobler spirit;
Of these not least the dauntless three, who broke
Through hostile ranks, and drew from Bethlehem's well
Its deep, cold water for their thirsting leader;
Miriam and Deborah, and Jephtha's daughter
Whose high heart yearned with virgin loves and
    longings;
Who mourned its bright, its broken dreams, yet gave
Her sweet young life in willing sacrifice;
Fulfilling thus the rash vow of her sire;
Sealing his victory with her unstained blood.

Nor less was stirred the soul of Sulamith
By many a thrilling tale her father told her
Of deeds of prowess he himself had seen,
Or deadly hazards, glorious victories
In which he bore a part. And so his hand
Swept all her spirit's chords, and woke within her
The symphonies of lofty sentiments—

Devotion, loyalty and reverence,
Enthusiasm for the sacred right,
And passionate love of truth and purity.
And oft she voiced them in the matchless songs
Of Israel's poet king, oft in her own,
That blended with the caroling of birds,
The plash of waters and the moaning winds;
But sometimes rose in rich and pealing notes,
That drowned all else in floods of melody.

Thus stole away the smoothly gliding years;
Then, to the sky that long had brightly smiled,
There came the dread, inevitable cloud,
Which hides, within its ever darkening folds,
The thunderbolt that only bides its time
To rive and shatter earth's securest joys.

At near approach of wintry storms, again
The household of Amminadib had sought
The comforts of their sheltered city home;—
All but the Syrian sons, who staid behind
To guard the house and flocks on Lebanon.
Amminadib, as oftentimes before,
Had wrought some public service for the king,

With that intensity with which he always
Labored or fought or urged his chariot's flight.
The task accomplished, a strange weariness
Had overcome him, and a sudden pang
Shot through him like the piercing of a sword.
It passed away and was forgotten quite,
But came again ere many days had passed;
And yet again, a sharper agony,
No longer yielding now to remedies
That hitherto had given prompt relief.
He knew it was the last, and calmly spoke
His farewell words to the belovéd ones
Who with their tears and prayers had fain detained him,
But whose dear faces faded from his sight,
While other, brighter visions, that should fade
No more forever, dawned upon his soul.

As at the tomb of Christ, even so two angels—
The one named Memory and the other Hope—
Stand at the tombs of all whose lives have been
Like Christ's in their self-sacrificing love,
Their truth and purity, to speak the words
Of consolation, that so much assuage
The mourner's grief, and wholly take away

Its bitterness and gloom.  One casts the sweet
And healing recollections of the past
Into its fountain ; and the other makes
The very tears which from that fountain flow
Resplendent with a brightness not of earth,—
The brightness of anticipated joys,
That Heaven shall richly yield, when severed hearts
Shall find each other there, to part no more.

With her twice widowed, and with Sulamith
In this her first experience of grief,
These angels twain abode, and ever whispered,
"Why weepest thou?" to one or to the other,
As, at the touching of some hidden spring,
Fresh floods of tears would rise and overflow.
But when the wintry months, so sadly bleak,
At length were gone, and the bereavéd ones
Again had sought their home on Lebanon,
All its associations seemed so fraught
As with the unseen presence of the dead,
They ceased to feel that he was wholly gone,
And more and more their hearts were comforted.

## IV.

## DAWN.

ANOTHER year had sped.   Returning spring
Had softly breathed upon the wintry world,
And all its icy rigors flowed away ;
Then o'er earth's nakedness a new-made robe,
Of tender green and interwoven flowers,
Was magically spread.

The wakening life
Thrilled the responsive heart of Sulamith.
The rising tides of health and joyfulness,
The rich unfolding rose of womanhood,
Her tall and graceful form, like queenly palm tree ;
The flowing tresses of her silken hair,
The flush that brightly bloomed upon her cheeks—
Tinged by the summer sun's too ardent gaze—
The kindling of her darkly liquid eyes,

*Sparkling or melting like the Syrian dove's,
Her smooth, calm forehead and her lips of sweet-
    ness,
But, chief of all, the informing grace within,
Of mind and soul which found their meet expres-
    sion
In every motion, feature, tone and look ;—
Such were the blended traits and elements
That shaped her into virgin loveliness,
Fairer than e'en the fairest flowers of spring,
Which beautified the slopes of Lebanon.


As hung the setting sun above the peaks
Of purpled mountains looming in the west,  .
A huge, dilating mass of spheréd gold,—
Beside the rocky basin, Sulamith
Alternately beheld the tossing waters,
And the rich splendors flooding all the plain.
But, for a space, her questioning eye was turned
To scan an unfamiliar flock, that came
Within her vision's scope,—the sheep and shepherd
Alike made golden by the alchemy

---

* See Dr. Burrowe's Commentary on the Song of Solomon.

Of sunset glory. Thus absorbed and musing,
A voice, deep-toned and richly musical,
Broke through her revery; and, looking up,
She met the gaze, intently fixed upon her,
Of one whose face perplexed her with the feeling—
A vague impression as of faded dream—
That she before had seen it; where or how,
She struggled to determine, but in vain.
At her first rapid glance she, meanwhile, noted
His manly stature, yet his youthfulness;
How dignified his bearing, yet what light
Of kindliness beamed from his searching eyes.
Above his high and massive brow his locks
Were thickly clustered, black as raven's wing.
His finely molded and expressive features
Were such as fully matched her high ideal
Of beauty that might well befit a hero.
"One of the youthful nobles of the land!"
Was first her thought; but this his garb denied,
Which differed not in texture or in fashion
From that a shepherd youth might meetly wear;
Therefore, "A shepherd!" was her next conclusion,
"Perhaps, belonging to the passing flock,
And, possibly, its owner's son or kinsman."

No shepherd's crook was in his hand. Instead—
More than his hand could grasp—a bulky package
Of gathered grasses, plants and early flowers,
And tiny branches of rare shrubs and trees,
Together bound and borne by loopéd cord.
With due obeisance made, he simply asked
For leave to quench his thirst, and highly praised
The fountain's beauty and the limpid water.
Warm blushes irrepressible suffused
The face of Sulamith as she responded,
And put into his hand a silver cup,
Brimming and dripping with its crystal contents,
Which eagerly he quaffed, and thanked the giver,
As though he had received a priceless boon.
And then, as loath to close the interview,
He questioned her of mountain summits near,
And streams that gleamed on the adjacent plain,
Or of the flocks, the vineyards and the orchards;
Then showed to her the treasures he had gathered
In his far mountain rambles through the day.
From these he culled some flowers he deemed the
    fairest,
And begged that she would keep them till they
    faded,

In memory of the wearied, thirsty stranger
To whose refreshment she had ministered.
And so the talk ran on, with some bright sallies
Of wit and merriment, which, though so lightly
Thus bandied back and forth between the two,
Were yet the shuttles that were firmly weaving
An unseen web, the warp and woof of which
Their kindred hearts supplied.

Thus, all too soon,
The bright hour passed, and brought its parting
time.
The stranger's form to Sulamith was lost
Upon the shadowed path ; but all night long,
Still by the fountain—in her dreams—the two
Held happy converse, till the morning light
Dispelled the sweet illusion. But, as though
It was the fitting sequel to her dream,
There rose, from far below, upon the air,
These ringing words, in which she recognized
The voice whose music had begun to wake
Its echoes in her soul :

## SONG.

The reddening sky
  Is heralding day ;
Rise, O belovéd !
  Come, fair one, away.

The winter is past ;
  Gone the chill rain ;
Spring broods over earth,
  And flowers bloom again.

Well do the birds know
  Their time to rejoice ;
On the still air floats
  The dove's cooing voice.

The fig tree its figs
  To ripeness refines ;
And fragrance distills
  From blossoming vines.

The mountains have caught
  The glow of the skies ;

Wake, my belovéd ;
  My fair one, arise !

From clefts of the rocks,
  Thy dwelling place high,
Oh, hither, my dove,
  With love's fleetness fly !

Smile, beautiful face,
  Again, smile on me,
And thrill me, sweet voice,
  With love's melody.

# V.

## LOVE.

TO Sulamith there never was a morn
    So rarely beautiful; never was light
    So softly golden, or the songs of birds
So rich in melody, or whispering breezes
So balmy with the breath of spring or laden
With such sweet fragrance of the dewy flowers.
The stranger's unforgotten words still thrilled her;
Her waking thoughts were haunted by her dreams;
And ceaselessly the music of his song,
That broke their spell, kept ringing in her ears.

    Deem it not strange, that thus the plant of love—
Oft now of slow and hesitating growth—
Should spring with tropical luxuriance,
Beneath the warmth of oriental skies,
And nearer to the fresh simplicity

4                            

That beautified the morning of the world
Than these its dimmer hours of far-spent day.


Yet Sulamith well knew a maiden's heart
Should not be lightly won. With much self-scorn,
She viewed the sudden tumult into which
An interview so brief with one unknown
Had somehow stirred her; and she chid herself,
With sharp severity, for the weak fondness
With which she dwelt upon his words and smiles,
That would have been the same, she doubted not,
Had any other maiden chanced, as she,
To give him drink when thirsty, or to heed
Too eagerly his pleasant courtesies.
'Twas but a passing fancy, and would go
As causelessly and fleetly as it came.


Thus with her well-trained judgment and a will
Strong by inheritance, she schooled her heart
And sealed her lips on what she deemed her folly;
And as, in spite of all this self-repression,
The plant of love kept growing more and more,
Its tender buds unfolding into blossoms
Of rose-red hue and perfume passing sweet,

She pulled them from their stems, and, half in pity
And half in anger, tore apart their petals
And flung them to the winds ; nay, would have plucked
From out her heart the plant itself which bore them,
But that the very thought was deadly pain.

Her elder brothers greatly loved the chase,
And now—the tasks of early spring performed—
Were scaling mountain-steeps, or plunging far
Into their deep recesses, seldom trod
By ev'n adventurous feet,—Amana's top,
Shenir's and Hermon, and the lions' dens
And lairs of leopards. From their practiced hands,
Of strength and skill that long-trained warriors
Might well have envied, sped the hurtling spear,
Or from their twanging bows the barbed arrows,
That bore swift death to the fast-fleeing game,
And e'en brought to their feet the pierced gazelle
From overhanging cliff, that towered above
All but its rare capacity to climb,
Or stretch of eagle's or of arrow's flight.

When, after days of absence, they returned,
With prey well laden, and with many a tale

Of perils 'scaped and triumphs hardly won,
Warm was their praise of one they chanced to meet
In their excursion, and with whom they shared
The pleasure of their manifold exploits.
Long did they dwell upon his strength and beauty,—
How much he knew of wood-craft, but how small
His skill or practice in the huntsman's art;
And yet how ready and how apt to learn:
And how the keenness of his wit, his jests,
His ringing laughter, and his well-told tales
Had made the days, while he was their companion,
To fly so fast they sorrowed at their close.
He had not chanced to tell to them his name,
And something in him—what, they could not say—
Had held in check their curiosity.
They only knew he sojourned with the shepherds
And vineyard-keepers of the king's possessions,
At Baal Hamon, which was some leagues distant,
Upon a sunny slope of Lebanon.

    An eager auditor was Sulamith;
But silent, for she doubted not that he
Her brothers praised was he on whom her thoughts
So fondly dwelt.  Hence, more than ever glowed

The hidden flame, and more profusely grew
The blushing flowers, that from their stems no longer
Were rudely torn and scattered to the winds.
Nor was it long before she heard again
The voice too well remembered and beheld
The form and face she never could forget.
Not wholly now a stranger, as at first,
He came.  Her brothers gave him hearty greeting ;
And, more than words, her mother's smile bespoke
A kindly welcome; and her own low voice—
Which, through a resolute exercise of will,
Told nothing of the throbbings of her heart—
Spoke fittingly her frank corroboration.

      The evening meal was spread, with viands
        choice
And plentiful, though simple,—luscious fruits,
Butter and milk of kine, with bread and honey,
And steaming venison of savory odor ;—
For answering appetites that mountain air
And exercise had whetted into keenness.
The guest, when hospitably urged to share it,
Showed pleased assent, but still a moment paused,
With slight embarrassment, and thus he spoke:

"Good friends, your kindness makes me much
    your debtor,
And surely claims that you at least should know
Something of him on whom it is bestowed.
The name of *Jedidiah which I bear—
Given by one whose partiality
Its meaning far too plainly indicates—
Is illy mated with my scant deserts,
And so presumptuous or self-flattering seems—
Though earnestly I crave the hinted blessing—
That I bespeak a humbler appellation.
Call me, I pray, 'the youth of Baal Hamon.'
Or, since I sojourn with the shepherds there,
And since my father was a shepherd boy,
And, in his riper years, a flock has tended
Less tractable than sheep, let me be known
But as "the shepherd," or 'the shepherd's son.'
This only do I further need to say:
It is my privilege to claim such kinship
With you, the household of Amminadib,
As our joint tribal place in Judah gives."

*Beloved of the Lord.

Well pleased were all, and friendship's arms
    at once
Were opened to receive him, while there burned
A warmer feeling in the maiden's heart,
Which secretly resolved, that the dear name,
So modestly renounced by him who bore it,
Should be its hoarded treasure, though her lips
Might frame themselves to lightly speak another.
So from that hour she always called him "shep-
    herd,"
While, in her heart, she whispered "Jedidiah,"
And with the love divine allied the human.

When ended the repast, at which they lingered,
In rare enjoyment of its social cheer,
The richer feast of genial fellowship,
Of kindred souls unsated, still went on :
Then in a parting psalm of joyous praise,
To Him who is the fount of life and good,
Their voices blended, with the accompaniment
Of harp and viol.  Then the shepherd spoke
His thanks and his farewell, ere he departed
To seek his lodging in the shepherd's tent,
Pitched at the mountain's base.  To Sulamith,

More than his words, his lingering gaze had spoken
That which again gave sweetness to her dreams.

His parting look and others of its kind,
Through which his soul had flashed intelligence
Of feelings that were kindling in its depths,
Availed to put to flight the self-contempt
With which, before their revelations came,
The heart of Sulamith had vainly sought
To quell the love that, without warrant due,
Had seized its citadel and held possession.
True, she could never build on looks alone
A confidence so strong that she would show—
At least show purposely—responsive feeling,
By single answering glance or tell-tale blush.—
Not so, if eyes, or blood that surged within,
Would acquiesce in strictest guardianship
And planned repression by the regnant will,
Should her sweet secret ever be betrayed.

But why should love of what is lovable
Be scorned or questioned, e'en in giving all,
And for its lavishment receiving naught?
What knows or cares the earth or sea or sky,

Enrobed with morning's beauty, of the thrills
Of rapturous admiration waked thereby—
And without fault—in nature-loving hearts?
The pictures which her father's hand had drawn,
In living colors, of the great and good,
Were hung upon the walls of her soul's chambers,
And almost idolized as bright ideals
Of what in life is noblest, loveliest;
Yet was she not ashamed to realize
That no reflection of her deep devotion
E'er on her shone from their unchanging features.
And why might not her heart as blamelessly
Render the tribute of its love to him
Who, in his living self, for her embodied
Like winning traits of grace and nobleness,
E'en though, for all its lavished treasures, he
Should yield her no return or recognition?

    The days, the weeks, went by, and still the
        shepherd—
So let him now be called—was seen no more
When passed in sight the flocks of Baal Hamon.
The brothers only knew that he had been
Suddenly summoned to Jerusalem,

And that it was his purpose to return
With such dispatch as might be in his power.
The bloom of Spring was gone, and Summer's fervors
Had scorched its lingering herbage; yet he came not.
No word of Sulamith deplored his absence;
But, o'er the mountain slope and the wide plain,
Far as her eye could note the passing forms,
She watched, day after day, with eager hope
That he for whom she longed would be among them;
Yet, though so vainly, neither look nor sigh
Gave outward token of her disappointment.
The cheerful patience of her love and trust
Unfaltering stood the tests that sorely tried it;
And daily tasks so filled her hands and thoughts,
That scanty room was left for weak repining.
And, oftentimes, a wondrous gift she had,
For peopling solitude with the creations
Of vivid memory or imagination,
Filled all the nooks of home and mountain haunts
With images of the beloved departed.
Among her spirit's visions, she beheld
The shepherd's face and form, and, with the ear
To which all silence speaks, would hear again
The music of his voice in speech or song.

Once, near the sunset of a busy day,
At which the heat of the advancing season
Was gratefully tempered by the cooling air,
Upon her rocky seat beside the fountain,
She sat with half-closed eyes that scarcely noted
The flashing segment of the sinking sun;
Nor, in her deep absorption, did she hear
The sound of footfalls that were close at hand;
To all oblivious, till a thrilling touch,
A hand laid on her own, dissolved the spell,
And tender, pleading, unforgotten tones,
Which almost hushed the beatings of her heart,
And, notwithstanding all she had resolved,
Sent to her cheek and brow its crimson tide,
Made music of the sweet name Sulamith.
But scarce a moment was she left to feel
The flush of maiden shame at this betrayal
Of her heart's secret, caused by her surprise.
The Shepherd,—he it was,—as though he saw not
Her beautiful confusion, or because
He was too manly to avail himself
Of an unfair advantage, gave, at once,
In these warm words, that yet were humbly spoken,
Full utterance to his feelings, long restrained:

"Oh, Sulamith, when first I met thee here,
'T was thy dear hand which, from these pure, cold
waters,
Gave me the sparkling draught that quenched my
thirst;
But even while its seasonable refreshment
Assuaged the fever of my blood and brain,
My soul grew conscious of a deeper want,
And every lingering hour that since has followed
Has made it but the more importunate;
And now, intense and irrepressible,
It drives me to the fountain whence alone,
Its passionate craving can be satisfied.
As desert wanderers for water thirst,
So thirsts my soul, oh Sulamith, for thee."


For one brief moment of bewilderment,
And rapid rallying of her scattered thoughts,
And dawning certainty, that what she saw
And heard and felt was not a blissful dream,
Her lips were silent and her eyes were downcast;
Then, with instinctive grace, and artlessly,
She dipped her silver cup into the fountain,
As she had done that memorable eve,

And filling it again to overflowing,
She softly said, or rather seemed to say,
More through the sweet significance of look
And attitude and proffered draught, than low,
Scarce uttered words, "Let him that thirsteth drink !"

One joy of Eden, Eden's loss survived,
And through the gate went with the fallen pair,
Ere o'er that gate was set the cherubim
And flaming sword, to keep the way of life.
Oft still it seems untouched with blight of sin,
And oft it works enchantment, bringing back
To earth anew the vanished Paradise,
Its mellowed brightness and its odorous air,
Its parted streams that flow through lands of gold,
And precious stones—or are they flashing dew-drops,
On its fresh verdure and unfaded flowers?—
This joy of Eden is the joy of love
When first enkindled in responsive hearts
Of those not fallen from early innocence.
Such love, with flowers so pure and delicate,
Unhandled and unsullied, and with fruits
On which the bloom yet lingered undespoiled,
Filled with an overflowing blessedness

The heart of Sulamith and his whom now
She called her Shepherd, and, in tenderest thought,
Named Jedidiah, of the Lord beloved.


Oh, story old as is humanity!
Yet not outworn, forever freshly new;
And oh, experience, common as is heart
That answereth to heart in man and woman
Of every generation, every clime!
But with its more than myriad variations,
Each one a special charm, a rare delight;
Nor ever more so than was realized
By these on whom love's roseate light had dawned
With such surpassing brightness, that it seemed
Above all Lebanon's glory and the world's,
Flooding their souls with rapture as unique,
Novel and vivid as they might have felt,
If, like the two thrilled hearts that waked in Eden,
They were the first and only who had learned
The secret of its wondrous blessedness.


Soon they among whom these enchanted ones
Mingled in life's familiar intercourse,
Knew of the change that could not be concealed,

So visibly the gladness which it wrought
Beamed from their faces, breathed in all their words,
And floated on the air in happy songs.
But Sulamith at once had sought her mother,
And with her glowing face hid in her bosom,
Had told the tender tale. It deeply stirred
The sympathy of that fond mother's heart;
And brought quick tears, that partly were of joy
And partly sorrow, at the memories
Of kindred scenes and feelings of her own,—
Sweet dreams of life's fresh morn, all, long ago,
So rudely broken and forever fled.

  The summer, with its ripening fruits and
 harvests,
And withering heat of blazing suns, from which
The ever cool retreats and breezy steeps
Of Lebanon unfailing refuge gave,
Was hastening to its close. Think not of all
Its fleeting days to love's endearments given;
Both Sulamith and he she called her Shepherd
Had fitting work to do, and it was done
Faithfully in its season. All their converse
Was not of love alone. Far other themes

Oft held their earnest thought nor failed to give
A tireless charm and zest to their communion.
The shepherd brought, for mutual inspection,
Rare treasures gathered from the woods and fields,
And nature's wonders, nature's beauties more,
Stirred all their souls to praise and tenderness,
And blended awe and love for nature's God.
Thus wisely, worthily diversified,
The sweetness of their daily intercourse
Grew more intensely sweet, yet never cloyed.
But when is earthly happiness complete?
Some nameless apprehension or unrest,
Some cloud, invisible to other eyes,
E'en to the heart that basks in golden beams,
Nor knows it may not evermore rejoice, ·
Will bring a passing shadow unexplained—
A vague and dream-like sadness, simply felt,
Not understood. And so with Sulamith:
At times to her a strange foreboding came,
Or sense of mystery that might at last
Unfold the secret that would bring her woe.

Once, when this mood of sadness and of doubt
Had causelessly swept o'er her, she espied,

On the declivity, not far below,
And nearer than the flock and his companions,
The Shepherd passing by. Impulsively,
With beat of timbrel and with rythmic words
To which the plaintive music lent a pathos
Beyond their simple meaning—thus she signaled
Appealingly the sadness of her heart:


### SULAMITH'S CALL.

Tell me, belovéd, where feeds thy flock?
And where, in shadow of tree or rock
Or grassy dell, shall its resting be?
For fain, with it, would I follow thee.
Ah, why, when the sheep thou leadest hide
From the driving storm or the hot noontide,
Should I be as one that turns aside,
As a wanderer who has no share
In the shepherd's tender love and care?


Scarce had her sad song into silence died,
Ere, like an echo, but in utter contrast
With its deep mournfulness, joyous, exultant,
Rang the response that brought her reassurance:
5

### THE SHEPHERD'S ANSWER.

If, oh, thou fairest of women, indeed,
Thou knowest not whither my flock I lead,
Then after its footsteps follow fast ;
And, before the noontide hour is past,
The tent of the Shepherd thou shalt see,
Under the shadow of rock or tree,
Or in grassy dell, awaiting thee !
And none, oh, best beloved, shall share
As thou in the shepherd's love and care.

## VI.

## SOLOMON.

THE robe of Summer, the bequest of Spring,
　　That in her yet unwithered beauty died,
　　Of fresh, deep green and garniture of flowers,
And wreathing roses blown each dewy morn,
Was now worn threadbare, and was colorless,
Dusty and soiled and tattered by the winds;
While broad, bald spaces of the hills and plains
Were left in their unsightly nakedness.

But not with summer's early flowers had faded
The love of Sulamith; for, through all changes,
Changeless it grew, perennially it bloomed,
And with unwasting fragrance filled her soul.
Yet, with the autumn's soft and dream-like haze,
And charm of pleasing sadness in the air,
There brooded over her a kindred feeling,
A melancholy which was void of pain
Or bitterness, and sweeter far than joy

That blazes fitfully in loveless hearts.
Gone was the living presence from her side
That most of all had made the summer bright.
Alone she walked among the leafless vines,
And trees that glowed with ripening autumn fruits;
Fond, joyous memories her sole companions,
Save as these changed to longings and regrets.

The shepherd had been summoned yet again
On urgent business of serious moment;
But not, as heretofore, was his departure
So sudden, but that ample time was left
For some last, lingering words with Sulamith,
And pledges oft repeated, sweetly sealed,
That in due season they should meet again,
And then—glad hope—the happy meeting be
To which death only should its parting bring.

A shadow of impending change, meanwhile,
Had spread and deepened over all the land;
For Israel's greatest king and conqueror,
Though scarce were spent his three-score years and ten,
Was slowly drawing near the dreaded end
Of his eventful life and glorious reign.

The final breaking of his matchless strength,
Though prematurely, had not strangely come :
For, with the exception of ten peaceful years
Before the close, and in his early youth,
The utmost vigor of his mind and frame
Had ceaselessly been tasked, in mortal struggles
With ever-rising storms that beat upon him.
And, more than all of these, his one great sin,
Remorse and wounded pride and hopeless griefs
Which, to the last, flowed from this bitter spring,
Had drained his energies and quenched the light
Of hope and courage which, till then, had shone
As guiding stars undimmed on darkest skies.

His virgin daughter, passing fair and dear,
Was worse—oh, worse unspeakably—than slain
By her own brother, David's first-born son,
And he in turn struck down by her avenger,
The favorite Absalom for beauty famed ;
Then this now heir apparent to the throne,
Too readily forgiven, and restored
To high position in his father's court,
Unschooled to patient waiting for the fruit
So sure to fall into his eager hands

At its fast golden ripening ; seizing on it,—
A traitor and a would-be parricide,—
Fell headlong from the height to which he clomb,
And met his righteous doom, but broke the heart
That o'er him yearned with deathless love, through all.


  Some gleams of consolation must have cheered
The chastened monarch's deeply contrite spirit,
When came at last his closing years of peace,—
Mild sunset rays after a day of storm,
The presages of an unclouded morrow ;
And something near to joy he must have known,
In giving all his unspent energies,
In lavishing his own long-hoarded treasures,
And gathering from the tribes of Israel
And tributary nations, fitting stores
Wherewith to build and beautify the Temple,
That like a crown of gold, thick set with gems,
Should shine on Mount Moriah's rocky brow ;
Already planned by its great Architect,
But only to be reared by one whose hands
Had not been stained, as his, with crime and blood.

  With this completion of his closing task,

Sudden collapse of interest and vigor
Together followed; and the aged king,
With wearied head reclined, and folded hands,
And welcoming heart, awaited dreamless sleep;
And many a patriot Israelite, perplexed,
Pondered the question: "Who shall be his heir?"
Amnon and Absalom gone, left Adonijah,
Who, all men fully knew, was to himself
The heir expectant; and if goodliness
Of form and feature right and fitness gave
To wield the sceptre of a Saul and David,
Then had his lofty claim unchallenged stood;
But rashness, shallowness and self-conceit
Are ever illy matched with princely grace.
There yet remained a younger of the sons,
He of the fair Bathsheba (frail as fair,
Of virtuous preference and answering life,
Faithful and pure, when not by others swerved;
But, as the reed that bends with every wind,
So weakly pliant to each stronger will).

In Solomon his mother's comeliness
Was blended with his father's manly strength,
Though in the blending possibly was lost

Something of beauty, doubtless more of vigor.
His youth was blameless, innocent his tastes,
And, better than the city's throng and turmoil,
He loved the mountains, forests, fields and streams;
And so, amid the healthful scenes of nature,
His body and his soul to largeness grew.
The scholar of his age and scientist,
He mastered all yet scantly written lore,
And eagerly he searched the open scriptures,
Whereon are traced the wonders and the glories
Of lands and seas and skies, the mysteries
Of human hearts and lives, of sin and God.
Nor ever aimlessly or selfishly
Were treasured up his gathered hoards of know-
　　　ledge;
He passed them through the alembic of his thought,
And stored the rich results for worthy uses,—
His own, his nation's, e'en the world's, the ages'.
And often in his glowing soul were born
The poet's dreams of beauty, and his songs
That artlessly and freely from him flowed,
As music-making rills flow from their fountains.

So had he early found an ample scope

For all rare gifts wherewith he was endowed,—
A kingdom of the soul, of range as wide
As sweeps imagination's tireless wing;
High reaching as aspirings after God;
Rich in all real sources of delight
And good for man, whate'er his state may be.
Nor sought he more than such high privilege,
As thus, with unblurred vision of his youth,
He for himself had recognized and prized
Above all price, and made his choice supreme.

Nathan the Seer, his teacher in the law,
His spiritual guide and swerveless friend,
Had early, in Jehovah's name, announced
That he should sit upon his father's throne;
And David, with unquestioning acceptance
Of the divine decree, had given Bathsheba
His solemn promise it should be obeyed;
But to none others, not even Solomon,
Was intimation of his purpose made.
Hence no disturbing dream of future greatness
Marred Solomon's contentment, or did aught
To thwart his simpler, nobler, grander aim.
Ah! better, happier, had it been for him,

If far from him forever had been kept,
Both dream and answering reality.

Only when Adonijah's mad attempt
To wrest the kingdom from his father's hands—
Ere on it death had loosed their failing hold—
Had brought precipitation of events,
And made imperative the proclamation
Of David's final choice, had Solomon
Known aught of what was purposed.  His life-scheme
Thus set aside, recoiling and oppressed
With sense of unpreparedness to rule
Over a kingdom to such greatness grown,
Yet meekly bowing to his father's will,
And well assured it was the will of God,
With many a prayer for help in his felt weakness,
He took, reluctantly, the offered sceptre;
And so that long and peaceful reign began
Which reached a pitch of proud magnificence,
That waked the praise and wonder of the world,
And yet beneath its outward glory hid
The elements of sure and swift decay.

# VII.

## FORESHADOWINGS.

**N**OT as the electric flash that now transmits
　　Its record of events to distant lands,
　　Traveled the tidings of momentous change
Wrought in the sovereignty of Israel;
But, spreading and advancing, day by day,
As spread the circling ripples of a pool
From where it has been stirred by plunging stone,
They reached betimes to Lebanon's retreats;
And to the household of Amminadib
Brought sorrow for the mighty monarch's death.
But they rejoiced that in his room and stead
Reigned Solomon his son, famed through the land
For wisdom, goodness, grace and modesty,—
Virtues too rare among the royal brothers.

　　Scarce had subsided into wonted quiet
The brief commotion by the news aroused,

Ere at the cottage messengers arrived
Bearing the signet of the new-made king,
And with it his behests: The Syrian sons
Should take the management of his estates,
His vineyards and his flocks at Baal Hamon;
And from contiguous regions should collect
The royal revenues. And, furthermore,
It was the sovereign will of Solomon,
Nor less the dictate of his gracious heart,
That Sulamith the beautiful, their sister,
Should be his bride and sharer of his throne.

All were amazed, as if from cloudless skies
Had crashed a thunder-peal. The elder sons
Were much elated at their own promotion;
Nor doubted they the king's prerogative
To set aside, at his mere will and pleasure,
Their shepherd-friend's betrothal with their sister,
Which, as they knew, had not been ratified
By such accustomed usages and forms
As made betrothal, scarcely less than marriage,
Of binding force and sacred obligation.
Nor in his absence, now so far prolonged
Beyond the expected time for his return,

Had tidings reached them of his place or state.
If still he lived, some other comely maiden
Perchance had won his heart from Sulamith.
But be it as it might, the king's command
Left no alternative but to obey.

Least moved of all seemed Sulamith. Her face
An ashen paleness wore, but all its lines
Were rigid with the high and fixed resolve
Of her unfaltering soul. Ah, now she knew
Why shadows oft had dimmed her brightest dreams,
And phantom shapes, that warned of coming ill,
Haunted her waking thoughts from day to day.
Yet stood she as the house upon the rock,
On which, from thunder clouds, might torrents pour
And lightnings strike, but unavailing all
To shake the steadfastness of its foundation.
Her heart might break, but would not be untrue;
Her love and life could but together die.

Meanwhile the messengers in silence stood,
Waiting the brothers' answer; but their eyes
Had caught a look upon their sister's face
They dared not misinterpret. Still they hoped

That, possibly, delay might serve to bring
Some wavering of her purpose, yet too strong—
They plainly saw—to yield at sternest bidding.
Vainly! for Sulamith's true womanhood
Had, in the moment, grown to its full height,
And shaken off all artificial bonds
Of deference to man's supreme dictation,
In questions that concerned her woman's heart.

      The brothers simply, with profound obeisance,
Their loyalty avowed and readiness
To do the king's commands.  Then Sulamith
In suppliance bowed before the messengers,
And thus her blended prayer and purpose spoke:

      "Behold, the handmaid of the king, who waits
To be or do whatever he requires,
Save in the things which God and right forbid.
That she has found such favor in his sight
Is marvelous to her, who is unworthy
To kiss his royal robe.  Oh, say to him,
That for the proffered honor she is grateful,
And with her life its memory shall live:—
The king is youthful and his tender heart

Could take no joy in that for which another's
Would bleed and break. The king is greatly wise,
And needs not to be taught how valueless
The shell without the kernel, or the body,
Though beautiful it were, without the soul.
Ah, what were name, sweet name, of bride or wife,
Apart from love to give it truthful meaning!
He asks what he has deemed a Lebanon flower
In its fresh, fragrant prime; but, from its stem
Plucked with rude hands, how soon its bloom would
      fade,
Its beauty and its perfume steal away!
Such withered, worthless flower were Sulamith
If severed from her love, which is her life;
Nor her's alone,—irrecoverably pledged
To one, who could not even for the king
Put back the changeless gift within her power."

And now the messengers—who could but see
How vain were further parleying—took their leave:
Then burst upon the head of Sulamith
The gathered storm her act and words had stirred
Within the hot hearts of her Syrian brothers,
Because, forsooth, they feared that Solomon,

Provoked at her refusal, would withdraw
The offices he had conferred upon them—
Far less, they shrewdly judged, to do them favor,
Than, through their help, to win their beauteous sister.

"Oh, damsel! rash and willful," said the eldest,
"Knowest thou what lightest doom may well be thine,
For thy perverseness? Thou shalt die unwed.
No husband call thee wife, no children mother.
Think not, the king whose power thou mightest
    have shared,
Will suffer thy lost shepherd, if e'er found,—
Or subject of his own or other realm,—
To seize the prize he vainly sought to win.
If not the favored bride of Solomon,
Then with his servants shall thy station be.
Scorning to sit with him upon his throne,
The kitchen of his menials thou mayest rule,
Or tend perchance his vines at Baal Hamon."

Thus flashed the lightning of their kindled
    wrath,
And swept the tempest of their scorching words,
Venting the wounded, keenly smarting sense

Of masculine superiority,
Which in the oriental bosom dwells.
But little harmed was Sulamith. Above
The windy storm her wingèd thoughts had flown.
Her loyalty and love and resolution
Had wafted her stirred soul to heights serene,
So that the angry brothers' cutting words
Had passed almost unheard. But when they ceased,
She felt the grateful silence, and withdrew,
To find it in her chamber, undisturbed.

Calmness like autumn's mellow, tranquil air
Followed the tempest, which had spent its rage
Upon the scarcely heeding maiden's head.
No repetitions followed. In the hearts
Of the late incensed brothers soon there rose
Fresh tides of pity and of tenderness,
As they recalled the accusing memory
Of their unkindness to their suffering sister,—
Their insults added to her deep distress.
Their every look and act was a confession—
Though by their lips unspoken—of the wrong.
Her mother's love and sympathy, as balm
Of Gilead, soothed her tried and wounded heart;

6

And He in whom she trusted evermore
A very present help in trouble proved.
And so she went her daily rounds of duty,
In thoughtfulness, but with such look of peace
As only comes to tried and trusting ones,
Who, tossed by storms upon a heaving sea,
Sure anchorage have found.

     Unwonted tumult
Had broken in upon the home's long quiet,
In consequence of Solomon's command.
"The business of the king requireth haste,"
Hence every hand must give its utmost aid
In furtherance of needful preparation
For the departure of the Syrian brothers,
To occupy the posts he had assigned them.

    And now the appointed day was drawing near
When these first fledglings of the household nest
Should spread their wings for flight.  Blent with
   the grief
Of those who loved them were anxieties
That o'er them swept, like shadows cast of clouds,—
Dread of the king's displeasure or persistence

In what he had declared his sovereign will;
To Sulamith the sense of mystery,
That ever deeper grew concerning him
She called her shepherd, but of whom she knew
Only that next to God he was her all,
And, whether still his place on earth were found,
Or death had claimed him, that her deathless love
Forever a reality must be.

The hurried tasks completed, in due time,
A restful hour had come; and Sulamith,
After brief musing, tuned and touched her viol,
Long silent; and soft melodies and sweet—
Wordless a while—were floating on the air.
Then came brief snatches of impromptu song,
Half joyful and half sad, woven of themes
Through which she lightly passed from gay to grave.
At last absorbed she seemed and as inspired—
But less with music's spell or poesy,
Than by the glowing purpose of her soul;
And, with quick strokes of passionate energy,
She swept the chords, and, in notes clear and high
As song of soaring lark, her words rang out:

Many waters cannot quench love ;
Floods to drown it powerless prove ;
All a man hath for love he may give,
Yet utterly scorned and loveless live.

At sudden pause of the song's vehement flow,
Before the singer's eyes, athwart the floor,
A shadow fell. The heart of Sulamith
Was for an instant thrilled with gladdening hope,
That he, for whom the yearnings of her soul
Were at full tide, perchance had come at last!
But one swift glance dispelled the fond illusion,
And sent the surging blood to cheek and brow,
As now within the door appeared a stranger,
And the confusing fear swept over her,
That he had overheard the words she sang.
His courteous salutation (into which
There entered not a hint, through word or look,
Of aught amiss) brought back to her, meanwhile,
Her scattered self-possession. But severely
Was tested soon what she had thus regained,
When presently he told her of his errand ;
For he had been deputed by the king
To bear his royal greetings and his mandates

Unto the household of Amminadib,
And, chiefly, to his well-beloved daughter.
His mission called for special urgency:
He therefore begged she would, without delay,—
Together with her brothers and her mother,—
Attend to the instructions which he brought
From Israel's king, the mighty Solomon.

Soon in his presence all were duly met,
And thus, in well-weighed words, the king's com-
    mands
Were briefly stated: All that, heretofore,
Had been his pleasure for the elder brothers
Was re-affirmed; and it was still his wish—
Only intensified by her refusal—
That beauteous Sulamith should be his bride.
Yet would he pledge to her his royal word,
That it should only be with her consent,
Freely and gladly given, if at all.
He asked and he commanded nothing more
Than her mere presence at Jerusalem,
Under her honored mother's watchful keeping;
And that for once at least he might behold her,
And she, if but for one brief moment, him;

And, with him, also look upon the face
Of him whose love she held above the king's;
Then freely make her choice, and it should stand.
An escort and provisions for the journey
Were furnished by the bounty of the king,
And now would shortly be at their command.

As when from shrouded sky, through one small rift,
The sunlight bursts, with radiance that seems
Brighter than even when for cloudless days
His unquenched beams are shed, so Sulamith—
Who long had walked upon a darkened path—
Saw, in a single hint of the king's message,
Its passing reference to the one she loved,
That which illumined all obscurity,
Scattered all doubts, and poured full floods of light
Upon her future, such as never shone
E'en in the noontide of her happier past.

The rest, in less degree, for varied reasons,
Shared in her joy, and, even more than she,
Hailed, in the gracious message of the king,
Relief from burdening fears of his displeasure.

All acquiesced in its imperative summons
To Solomon's presence of the maid and mother;
And for the change were due arrangements made.
Agar, still strong and gentle as of yore,
Though nearing fourscore years, should have in
    charge
The younger children in their mother's absence;
And in the brothers' stead—soon to assume
The offices appointed by the king—
Her faithful son, well fitted for the station
In rare capacity and diligence,
Should take the oversight of all beside.
Ere rose the sun of the succeeding day,
The words of peace were said; and on the road
That leads from Lebanon to Jerusalem,
The royal chariot which conveyed the twain,
Under an escort of twelve mounted men,
Was speeding in the frosty morning air.

# VIII.

## JERUSALEM.

SCARCE had the sun, descending, passed mid-
way
Between its noontide altitude and setting,
On the fifth day since Sulamith and she,
Who more than ever to her yearning heart
Was all that mother means, began their journey,
When, from a sudden turning in the road,
Jerusalem, its longed for goal, uprose
Before their kindling eyes.

As yet the city,
Though much enlarged by David through his reign
Of forty years, had not outgrown Mount Zion.
Upon its brow his cedarn palace stood;
And, in its rear, full many a towering structure
Of kindred style and of cöeval building.
One massive fortress, in its ruggedness,
Frowned from a rocky steep on all below;

88

And, to the westward, there might be descried
The antique housetops and the moldering walls
Which were the last decaying links that bound
Jerusalem to Jebus, which of old
Had place among the cities that were founded
After the flood, on the new-peopled world ;—
A seat of power to which e'en Abraham
Did homage, paying to its priest and king,
Mystic Melchizedek, the sacred tithe.

To those who from the chariot keenly gazed,
Continued scrutiny brought marks of change :
What seemed at first a ridge, uneven, broken,
Around the city, soon they saw to be
Its yet unfinished wall.  On Mount Moriah,
That from the valley, narrow, deep, flood-worn,
Uprose in front, a rugged precipice,
Were excavations for the temple's site—
Piled rocks and earth-heaps and unsightly seams,
That darkly gashed what once were grassy mounds
Or vine-clad terraces, or bright parterres
That in the distance glowed with flush of flowers.

But less the many changes thus beheld

Impressed the mother's mind, than one unseen
Touched, with sad sense of loss, her grieving heart;
And also to the eyes of Sulamith
An instant gushed an overflow of tears
As memory brought, with startling vividness,
Her father's form and face, forever hid
From all the places in Jerusalem
That once had known them, known them long and
　　well.
An instant only.  As on falling rain-drops
The sun, emerging from the scattering clouds,
Sheds the bright beams which make them sparkling
　　gems,
Soon to evanish from the freshened air,
So speedily to this her tender woe
Came the supplanting rapture of her soul—
The blissful prospect ready to become
Blissful reality, that he who long
Had only been with her in memory—
Her living love—amid the city's throngs,
Waited to give her welcome, and would speak
Once more the sweet assurances for which
Her heart was thirsting, as the flower at noon-tide,
That, drooping, mutely pleads for rain or dew.

Two of the chariot guards on coursers fleet,
Had forward sped, to give to Solomon
Due notice of the coming of his guests ;
And even now the thunder of his train
Broke on their ears, and clouds of rising dust,
Whirled by the wind, o'er-canopied the road,
And ever nearer drew. The youthful king,—
Wearing a crown of gold, with precious stones
Inwreathed, and by his mother's hand bestowed
On the bright morning of that gladsome day,
Clothed with the vestments suited to his state,
With thirty warriors on either hand,
Each girded with a sword and each renowned
For his exploits in battle, as his guardsmen—
Thus rode full royally, in royal car
Fashioned by Tyrian artificers ;
Its framework of the polished wood of Lebanon,
Its pillars silver and its seat of gold,
Cushions of Syrian purple and its sides
With ebony inlaid, its carpet woven,
And wondrously embroidered, by the hands
Of the fair daughters of Jerusalem,
From love to him they proudly owned their king.*

* See Dr. Cunningham Geikie's Hours with the Bible.

On swept the royal cavalcade, until
The two met in the roadway, face to face,
Then halted, side by side, wheel touching wheel,
The car of state that bore king Solomon,
The chariot of humbler workmanship
In which the mother and the maiden rode.

A dream-like spell to Sulamith had come.
The pageant but a brilliant vision seemed ;
Its forms and faces swam before her eyes
Confused and indistinct as are the fancies
Of fevered brain.  But, through the wildering maze,
One steadfast thought and purpose gave a measure
Of reasonable quest to her swift glance,
That only—in the sight of crown and splendor—
A kingly presence noted ; then o'er all
Made bootless search for him compared with whom
The mightiest of kings was nothing now,
And who, she fondly hoped, had been the first
To give the tender welcome on whose foretaste
Her soul, else weak and sad, had sweetly fed.
Then, in the sinking of her baffled hope,
As sinks in cloudy depths the only star
That for a little space saves earth and sky

From all-devouring gloom,—upon her ear,
In thrilling closeness, with the very breath
Of its sweet utterance warm upon her cheek,
Fell once again what seemed the voice of him
Who by the fountain side had called her name,
And in the low, deep music of his tones
Had shrined it sacredly and evermore.

"Oh, God of Israel!" she would have said,
But that her lips were tremulous and failed
To frame the rising fear that sought expression—
"Oh, God of Israel!" she wildly thought,
"Has this weak heart so lost its hold on Thee,
So willfully allowed its poor, vain longings
To fill and sway it, of Thy will forgetful,
That I at last in righteousness am left
To fond delusions, mocking fantasies,
And dreams of madness, deemed realities?"

Great Solomon, the king himself, it was,
Who from his car had leaned and gently spoken
The name of Sulamith, to her who heard
As though she heard not. Reason had not fled;
It was no vain illusion ; not alone

The Shepherd's voice;—in that, in all, the shepherd!
Who though of princely station yet had worn
The garments which pertain to those whose rank
In life is lowly; and on Lebanon,
With such had sought and found companionship;
Humbling himself that he might be exalted,
And dowered with wisdom's more than golden gains;
And that, apart from all the trammeling ways
Of royalty, in nature's chosen haunts,
Her calm retreats, her silent solitudes,
She might the more to him reveal her beauty,
And to his searching eye make deep disclosure
Of all the marvelous mystery of her life.

      Backward he waved the guardsmen, quite
      beyond
The hearing of his voice, and where their eyes
Might illy serve their curiosity;
And from their charge dismissed the charioteers;—
No movement fearing of the well-trained steeds,
Until the reins again were in their hands;—
And then with warmly pleading tones he cried,
"Look, Sulamith, upon thy king, who might
Speak with authority and by his power

Enforce obedience to his sovereign will;
But who in humble suppliance begs the boon
On which his happiness, his very life,
Or all that makes it worthy of the name,
Depends.  He lays his sceptre at thy feet,
And prays that thou wilt reign his bosom's queen.
Or dost thou still to thy first purpose cleave,
To be the shepherd's bride?  Then have thy choice.
Thy chosen waits to hear from thy sweet lips
Its final confirmation."

     Then the king
Took off his crown and laid his robe aside,
His outer robe with many a gem adorned,
Laced and embroidered with a wealth of gold;
And lo, before the eyes of Sulamith,
In which the happy tears were glistening,
He stood in shepherd's guise, as when he wooed
And won her deathless love on Lebanon!

   Her lips in vain essayed to make reply;
But in the mantling glow upon her face,
Suffusing all its pallor, as the rose
Of sunrise all the dimness of the dawn;

And in the tender light that shone through tears,
Which on the long, dark fringes of her eyes
Gathered, like drops of morning dew on flowers,
He read the voiceless answer of her soul.

Something beside her glad affirmative
His searching eye discerned.   He also saw
That mingling with the brightness of her joy
And deepening beneath his ardent gaze,
Were shadows of misgiving, and of doubt
Lest he she most had honored were not true;
Since he had come to her with garb and name
That now she could but fear had falsified
His real selfhood and his princely state.

Hence Solomon, who felt the subtle change
That o'er her face had swept—as o'er the fields
The sunlight's faint obscuring which is wrought,
By slightest film of cloud, scarce palpably,—
As though his quickened sense divined its meaning,
Spoke of his late sojourn amid the wilds
Of Lebanon, and told how he, who thought
An elder brother would ascend the throne
Upon his father's death, had sought for wisdom,

More than for beaten gold or priceless rubies;
And how in its pursuit he left the court
And dwelt in distant parts with common men,
As one with them, that so he might the better
Learn of their ways and gain the useful lore
So often hidden from the proud and great;
And thus had chanced to come to Baal Hamon;
To all unknown, save to his faithful servant,
Who would have kept his secret unto death;
And how, in search of wisdom he had found
More than he sought, fair wisdom's fairer rival—
Found Sulamith, as wise as she is fair;
And learned that earth has nothing to compare
With the true heart that in her bosom dwells,
Or with the love that dwells in her true heart.
Far from him was the thought that his deception
Should do herself or others aught of wrong.
Nor had he falsely spoken when he claimed
Another name than that of Solomon;
For that he claimed was also his, its tenure
As sacred as the office of the prophet,
Nathan his partial friend, who had conferred it.

While yet with kindling eloquence he urged

7

His vindication, from the candid eyes,
In which he saw his truth and honor dimmed,
Beamed full acquittal ; and the thought of blame,
That on the face of Sulamith had quenched
Something of welcoming brightness, swiftly changed
Into a yearning sense of self-reproach,
Whence flowed afresh the streams of tenderness,
For healing of the hurt which she had done.

Over the scene which thereupon ensued,
While passed a little space of swift-winged time,
Oblivion's veil impervious is spread.

Then Solomon his coronet resumed
And robe of royalty.  Adown the slope
Of Olivet the chariots, side by side,—
The warrior guardsmen in the front and rear,—
Sped swiftly toward the wide-swung city gate,
Whence issued forth a bright-robed multitude,
A welcoming throng of Zion's stately maids,
The dark-eyed daughters of Jerusalem,
And thus with song the stayed procession hailed :

## CHORUS.

Who is he that cometh, in royal robes majestic,
And crownéd with the crown wherewith his mother
crowned him,
For the day of his espousals, and the gladness of
his heart ?

Who is he with chariot among the olives gleaming;
Above him floating cloudlike dense odors on the air,
Of gums and spices priceless, of frankincense and
myrrh ?

Who is she that looketh forth as the dewy morn-
ing ;
Fair as silvery moon, in its pathway through the
sky ;
In her beauty beaming, as the sun at noonday ;
Over all victorious, like a bannered host ?

## Invocation.

Awake! awake! oh, wind of the north;
  Come, south wind, over the garden blow,
Until from its flowers and spices forth
  Its perfumes far abroad shall flow;
And my belovéd one shall know,
      By the odorous air
      They have laden, where
The fruits that wait for his coming grow.


## Response.

I am come to the garden, sister-bride;
  I have gathered its fragrant spicery.
The feasts its luscious fruits provide,
  With honey and wine of love, I see
Spread in the garden shades for me,
      'Mid clustering flowers,
      'Neath rose-roofed bowers,—
Spread, oh, my soul's delight, by thee!

## IX.

## HALCYON DAYS.

T last the day of days for Sulamith
Had faded into evening's grateful shade,
That cooled her fevered brow and round
her drew
Its curtaining of silence and repose.
The king, in thoughtful kindness to his guests,
The mother and the maiden, overtasked
With days of journeying and exhausting strain
Of ceaseless cares, alternate hopes and fears,
And final flood of overwhelming joy,
Had left them early to the solitude,
The luxury of comfort and of rest
And guarded stillness of the spacious room—
Joint room and chamber—for their use assigned,
And in their honor furnished royally.

The level rays of the uprisen sun
Threw wakening splendors on the chamber walls ;

And Sulamith from deep and dreamless sleep
Emerged, with bounding life.  The happy thought
That lingered latest in her consciousness,
Ere it had sunk 'neath slumber's lulling wave,
Was first to greet its swiftly brightening dawn :
He who in shepherd guise had won her love,
To whom her fond and faithful heart had clung
Through dreary absence, deepening mystery,
And lures or threatenings that might have swerved
A will of less than swerveless constancy—
He from whom long her path had stretched apart,
Amid the shadows of uncertainty,
Had smiled upon her from their thickening gloom,
Had spoken in her ears again the words
That in her heart had glowed, while all without
Was dark and cold !

    And yet her bliss supreme—
As all earth's bliss—was not without alloy.
For rapturous moments, while aside were cast
The symbols of his majesty, her heart
Was almost satisfied, and still he seemed
What he had ever been amid the haunts,
The orchards and the vines of Lebanon.

But when again she saw him robed and crowned,
In all the grandeur of his royal state,
The vision that had burst upon her gloom
And seemed the full fruition of her hope,
Had faded, as a happy dream of night
Before the dull reality of day.

But though the brimming cup of happiness
Had somewhat lost of effervescent gleam,
Still was it passing sweet and still undrained ;
And when—before the flush of rosy morn
Had wholly left the mountains and the sky,—
He to whom all the currents of her soul
Were setting, as the rivers to the sea,
Stood in her presence, called her by her name,
In tones that made each syllable replete
With tenderest meaning, then her ebbing joy,
In full flood-tide, swelled to its overflow.

"My soul's belovéd ! peerless Sulamith !"—
Such was the salutation of the king—
"The freshened glow upon thy late pale cheeks,
The light that kindles in thy dove-like eyes,
Assurance give that night for thee hath wrought

Full reparation for the weariness
And waste of past exhausting, care-fraught days;
And from the sweetness of thy welcoming smile,
That on me once again unclouded beams,
My thrilled heart draws the gladdening confidence,
That if thy faithful love hath also slept,
It too hath found replenishment in sleep."


"Know thou that when I met thee, yester eve,
It was to claim thy pledge, fulfill my own,
And crown the day for which my soul had longed
With glad espousal rites, that would have made
Thee, best beloved, my bride.  But when my eyes
At last beheld thee, dearer than their light,
With something in thy looks before unseen,
A nameless charm which, more than beauty's bloom,
Drew all my soul to thee, then did I note,
With tenderness new-born, that like a lily
Which droops upon its stem in noonday heat,
Or scorching winds that from the desert blow,
So was it, love, with thee.  On thy pale face,
One moment bright with unexpected joy,
Deepened a shade of pained perplexity;
And all its wistfulness did plead with me

Against the eager impulse of my heart;
But now thy face is shadowless, thy smile
Unclouded as the sky of this clear morn;
Hence needless pity dies; my love is all;
And patience, that postponed the hour of bliss,
In kindness yesterday—the reason gone,
The morrow come—now pleads for its reward."

   Then Sulamith, with more than health's warm
     glow
Upon her face and bosom, made reply:

  "What thanks to thee I owe, that thou, beloved,
Did'st with my woman's weakness nobly bear,
Making thy strength its refuge, when my own
Availed not, in the tumult of surprise
And joy that blent with my unbidden fears.
Oh, well thou knew'st the truth my trembling lips
So vainly sought to speak; nor could'st thou doubt
The love that words were powerless to express.
And rightly now thou readest on my face
The bliss that brings oblivion to pain,
Once more to see thee, hear thy voice and know—
Though that were all—that thou thyself art near.
Yet, for thy sake and mine, I needs must ask

Thy further patient trust.  For thou art not
The shepherd only, he to whom my love
As such was fully, confidently given,
With whom I thought to journey side by side,
Equals in rank, congenial in aims,
In all things mated, on familiar paths.

"Would God thou wert but he to whom my
          pledge,
As life irrevocable, has been given!
Then at thy lightest word, without delay,
Should its fulfillment be.  It binds me still,
And shall forever;—dear and blessed bond!
Freedom from which would only bring me woe.
But, oh, belovéd, thou art Israel's king;
The world has not a loftier throne than thine.
No wings, as yet, have I wherewith to reach
The dizzy, shining height where thou hast flown,
But wings of love, and they are all untaught
The art of such high soaring.  Blameless so,
Thou needs must own, for they were trained by thee,
And only from thy teaching, further given,
Can ever venture the ambitious flight
Thy wishes urge.  Forgive me, if I seem

To answer lightly.  All my heart responds,
And all its loyalty pays reverent heed.
But for a shepherd's bride have I been schooled;
To this my wishes and my hopes have led;
And when, instead, there opens to my view,
All unprepared—as if to twilight shade
At once should come the dazzling light of noon—
A place beside the greatest of earth's kings,
Where I must match the glory of his state,
Must feel and do and be what it requires,
Wielding the influence that touches springs
Which may unlock, for realms and multitudes
And countless generations that shall be,
The treasury of blessings, or set free
Imprisoned woes and curses—wonder not
To mark the shrinking of my untried heart,
Or that, for more and higher than the sake
Of love or joy, whether of mine or thine,
I beg a little space in which my soul,
Bewildered by the suddenness and greatness
Of such a change, may seek its wonted peace,
And that with aid thou givest I may find
The wisdom, strength and meetness that I need
To do thy bidding and be wholly thine."

Thus far spake Sulamith, and then, abashed
And beautiful in virgin modesty,
At sudden consciousness that to her came
Of all the tender meaning of her words,
She turned away, and on her mother's breast
Sought sweet concealment for her crimsoned face
And starting tears which flowed, she knew not why.

A moment paused the king, a moment sped
A cloud of disappointment o'er his face.
One more,—while silent still,—his knitted brow
And compressed lip told of the strife within,
Between his baffled will and pitying love;
And then swift triumph hung its banners out
In softened light that kindled in his eyes
Through half-shed tears, and in the unshadowed smile
That o'er his features like a sun-burst swept,
As by the side of Sulamith he bent,
And, while his hand caressed her flowing hair,
Made gentle, generous answer to her plea.

" Fairest of women!—art thou wise as fair?—
Well might I question thy shrewd argument,
And by its consequence, itself disprove :

For lo, it brings the king, with whom to mate
Thou fearest, a suppliant to thy feet,
By thee enthralled through more than kingly power.
Thy wings—thou claimest—can make no upward
    flight;
But, plumed with noble thoughts, they bear thee now
Immeasurably above the common range
Of kingly exaltation; and thy sense
Of duty and of fitness which pertain
To royal station, show thee best endowed
With qualities that honor its possession.
But think not he, who loves thee as his soul,
Would press compliance with his fondest hope,
Against thy wishes or despite thy fears.
Enough that thou art mine, that thou art here,
That often in thy presence, in thy smiles,
Refuge and solace I may sweetly find
When wearied with the labors and the cares
That burden, or that vex the hearts of kings.
And rich the compensation for all loss
In brief deferring of expected bliss,
To be the trainer of my Lebanon Dove,
The happy teacher of these folded wings,
That, pliant to such loving tutorship,

Shall soon acquire the cunning and the strength
To waft their owner up to Israel's throne—
The nestling of his heart who sits thereon.

"Oh, honored mother of my plighted bride,
Witness her new-made promise to be mine;
And that my sacred, royal word is given,
That only she shall name the gladsome hour
When these betrothal vows shall be fulfilled.
But even now the audience hall is thronged
With multitudes who for my judgment wait.
Thanks, for this morning draught of blessedness
That yields refreshment for a toilsome day.
Jehovah watch between us while apart!
The strength of Israel your keeper be!"

Whether in mountain wilds or palaces,
Love works enchantment for its subject hearts,
All sounds attunes to their deep harmonies,
Over all scenes and objects brightly spreads
The beautiful illusion of their joy.
To Sulamith the peaceful nights were fraught
With rapturous dreams, and all the autumn days
Were golden, or so seemed, if skies were clear,

Or clouds inwrapt the pathway of the sun.
Yet lingered with her long, perplexing sense
Of strange environments, as though, awaking,
She gazed upon another world than that
On which her eyes had closed, when sealed for sleep.

A world of teeming life it proved, and all
In contrast with her past experience.
The palace halls, the chambers, and the court
Where fountains played, where still the turf was
 green,
And still the lingering flowers of autumn bloomed,—
Were often vocal with the blended sounds
Of pipe and timbrel, harp and psaltery,
And songs of worshipers or banqueters,
And peals of silvery laughter, musical
As notes of birds that hail the birth of spring.

Through latticed windows of the palace looked—
As pictures framed, transcendent ornaments
To deck the palace walls—full many a face
Of virgin youthfulness and beauty's bloom ;
And every sunny day, on the wide lawn
Or branching walks, were groups of merry girls,

Some palace denizens, and other some
The bright-robed maidens of Jerusalem.
And there were days when Sulamith herself
Appeared among them, stateliest of all ;
Then, as they flocked around her with their songs
And gay refrains of welcome and of praise,
To which with winsome grace she made reply
That ever aptly matched their sportiveness,
They seemed, with her compared, as clustering flowers
Gathered from fields and woods, indigenous,
And she the regal plant, exotic rare,
That filled the central space with crowning bloom.

When Sulamith had joined the groups of
    maidens,
Then oft, by opportune coincidence,
It chanced that Solomon, awhile released
From grave affairs pertaining to the realm,
Would watch, from overhanging battlement,
The joyous spectacle, and feast his ears
On the incessant babel of sweet sounds
That made monopoly of all the air.
And ever at such times he put away
Magnificence of oriental state.

Scarce aught beside his native majesty
Proclaimed him king. His youthful sympathy
With youthful mirth, inscribed upon his face,
Was known and read of all. Over the forms,
Of varied charms, that thronged the space below
His eye would sometimes sweep half carelessly,
Yet at its glance responsive faces brightened
And tuneful voices, in full chorus, rang
With glowing praise of his benignity.
But when, not long delayed, his searching look
Encountered her, who like the stately palm
Or citron in the midst of other trees
So in the midst of her companions stood,
His gaze was lingering, and between the two
Flashed messages that needed not poor words
For their interpretation.

                Festal days
Had ample space in Israel's calendar.
At their recurrence oft the banquet hall
By night resplendent shone with floods of light;
And all the air was heavy with perfume
And vibrant with the waves of melody;
While graceful virgins, with white arms upflung

8

And rythmic flight of lightly saudaled feet,
Threaded the circling mazes of the dance.
And from the gathered nobles of the land—
Joined also by the king—the hall would ring
With loud and long applause.  But Sulamith
Looked only once upon the brilliant scene,
Then turned away, with sadness and with shame,
And sense of outrage done to womanhood,
By profanation of her sacred charms.

So time sped on and scarce its flying wings,
E'en for brief moments, drooped with doubt or care ;
Love swept with tireless hand a harp of gold,
And made each resonant chord to tell of joy.
Nor were the tuneful lips of Sulamith
Unused to give meet utterance to her thoughts
And feelings, that, as streams from limpid springs,
Flowed forth in simple melodies like these :


### SONG.

I sing for joy that I am his and he mine, only mine ;
I quaff from ever brimming cup deep draughts of
    love's sweet wine.

His footfall, that I know so well, with bounding
    heart I hear;
And the odor-laden breezes are whispering, "He is
    near!"


The music of his name, that floats upon the con-
    scious air,
Is as the perfume that exhales from outpoured oint-
    ments rare.


Oh, why, thou best and noblest, why should it with
    wonder move thee,
That, for thy matchless loveliness, the virgins all
    do love thee?


Let but fall the smile that wins them, with a tender
    light on me,
And these feet, love-winged, shall bear me like a
    flashing ray to thee.


Oh, thou kingliest one, thy throne is upreared within
    my heart;
And in thy palace chambers, thou makest me dwell
    apart.

There, in overflowing gladness, I join my tuneful
  voice
With the maidens my companions, who in outer
  courts rejoice.

Together ring our choral songs with joy no reveler
  knows,
E'en when at royal banquetings choice wine unstinted flows;

For why, oh, why with jealous pain should the
  assurance move me,
That, for thy peerless loveliness, they also rightly
  love thee?

## X.

## QUESTIONINGS.

ALAS, for love's illusions when, too soon,
Confronted with life's stern realities!—
Like bubbles, beautiful with rainbow hues,
That float resplendent in the summer air,
Then touch some solid thing and are no more.

The clouds had gathered and the chilling winds
Had turned the driven rain to gleaming sleet,
When came to Sulamith faint whisperings
That in brief time to noisy rumors swelled,
And waked a tempest in the maiden's breast,
Compared with which the wintry blasts were balm.

The fierce, hereditary foe of Israel,
Ammon that on her eastern border lay,
By Joab's army, in King David's reign,
Conquered and crushed, and tributary now,

But turbulent and ever on the watch
To break the hated vassalage and take
Bloody revenge for Joab's cruelties—
The rumor said—was to be pacified,
And the two nations into concord drawn,
Through marriage of Solomon with * Naamah,
Daughter of Ammon's king, a princess famed
For loveliness that well befit her name.
So had the councilors of Solomon
Unanimously urged, and his consent—
It was affirmed—reluctantly been given.
To Rabbah, Ammon's rock-built capital,
Princely embassadors were on their way,
Charged with the king's commission, to conclude
The marriage treaty and convey the bride
Unto Jerusalem, in royal state.

An hour had come to storm-tossed Sulamith,
In which her anchorage had given way,
And left her drifting on a swollen tide
Of unquelled doubts and agonizing fears.

---

* Loveliness.

No trace of all the trouble of her heart,
Till then, had met the king's observant eye;
But now, as unannounced and suddenly,
Her room he entered, on her face beheld
The flowing tears, the pallor and the pain
Wherewith her inward woe was written there,
At once flashed on his mind, disturbingly,
Suggestion of the cause of her distress.

"My love, my soul's delight, what aileth thee?"
He asked, in tones full fraught with tenderness;
And waiting not reply, himself spoke on:

"I would that I had sooner sought to shield
My trembling dove from the envenomed tongues
That now I see have poisoned all her peace,
With false surmise of what has been decreed
Touching the kingdom and the hate of Ammon.
Hear from my lips the truth and dry thy tears:
The wise and mighty men my royal sire
Gathered around him and transferred to me,
To be the bulwarks of my throne, and aid
My yet unripened judgment, sorely taxed
With ever pressing questions on which hang

The nation's weal or woe, with one accord
Have given counsel, that firm amity
Be sought with Ammon's king, through my alliance
With Naamah his daughter; and to this—
The policy of which I question not—
Against my wish, I yield. But think not, thou
To whom are pledged my love, my life, my all,
That I have grown forgetful of my vow
To be thine, only thine. State marriages
To me are nothing more—the form, the name,
The realm's advantage or security;
The royal prestige, pomp and pageantry;
To gild with richer splendor Israel's throne;
To match its growing power, its widening fame
Among surrounding nations, over which
It needs must tower, in this and all things else,
Till in its brightening glory theirs is dim.—
Let it not startle thee, oh Sulamith,
To know that even ere my father died,
Through all the tribes of Israel and all
The tributary nations, messengers
Had sought for damsels dowered with beauty rare,
That, even as the fairest flowers are culled
From all the fields or gardens, they might grace,

With brighter bloom, the palace of his son—
His wives and concubines, with trains of virgins
Innumerous, their state to magnify.
But just as these were gathered, for like ends
The seas with nets are swept, the fields and woods
Laid under tribute for their fruit and game,
Their beasts of pasturage and fatted fowl;
And all, forsooth, to lade the royal board
With boundless plenty and variety.
Abundance fitly goes with kingly state;
But kingly wisdom, kingly self-restraint
Appropriate no more than well may serve
The simple, wholesome, common wants of man.
These virgins, all these wives and concubines—
Such only in the empty names they bear—
Are royal superfluities, or are
Mere palace-ornaments—the chapiters
That crown its pillars, knops and pomegranates,
The golden pendants and the wreathen work,—
That might not be, or might be torn away,
Yet wholly leave the sheltering home within,
Untouched in aught of comfort or of cheer.
They are the fringes on my outer robe;
But thou the silken garment that enfolds

My form with clinging closeness, and is stirred
With every throbbing of my love-thrilled heart.
To them, the many, it is mine to give
All thoughtful kindness, such as may insure
Their due contentment, health and happiness;
But oh, my treasured one, the one alone,
Choice one of her that bare thee, solely mine
Of all art thou, and such shalt ever be.''

With a new dawn of gladness in her eyes,
Its chastened light still struggling through her tears,
Thus Sulamith replied:

        '' Thy words, oh, king!—
Whom I must honor even as I love,
And whom to doubt were wretchedness untold,—
Thy words of reassurance, strong as sweet,
Dispel my fears and wholly fortify
My shaken trust, and yet they give me pain.
In every one of these of whom thou speakest,
These ornaments of palaces and thrones,
There dwells a woman's heart, such heart as mine,
That more than for the dainties of thy board
Or wines that for thy royal banquets flow,

Hungers and thirsts for love.  But only names,
Bare names, poor names, as empty as the wind,
Devoid of all their tender sacred meaning,
Shall meet the life-long restlessness and pain
Of nature's strongest craving in these hearts.
Oh, in the fulness of this blessedness
Which thou hast promised shall be mine alone,
Can I forget the hollow, pining hearts,
Which may not even feed upon the crumbs
That from the abundance of my table fall?"

But Solomon was silent, and to her,
In whose touched heart of keenest sympathy
Such questionings had risen, no answer came;
And painfully she felt that none could come.
Yet, not the less, her love, her passionate love,
Scarce blinded now, resistless, urged her on,
Vaguely dissatisfied, and wondering
What time would bring, and what the end would be.

The king still lingering with a clouded brow,
As though some vexing thought his peace had
    marred,
At length besought of Sulamith a song,

A parting song of love, from which perchance
His soul might sweetness draw for coming hours
That of her sweeter presence would be void.
And thus, in unison with what had passed,
With more of passion, less of melody
Than was her wont, these burning words she sang:

### SONG.

Set me as a seal upon thy heart;
   Bind on thee some token that I am thine;
Pledge me that none beside shall have part
   In the love to be forever mine.

Love is strong as death, and as the grave,
   So cruel the rage of jealousy;
Give me, belovéd, the boon I crave,
   And quenched its vehement flames shall be.

## XI.

## NAAMAH.

BRIEF was the reign of winter. Sullen skies,
  The bleak north winds, chill rains and
    pelting hail,
Flurries of snow and ice-commingled floods
Were of the past; and the returning sun,
Rekindling his abated fires, was now
Warming the air and wakening the earth
With thrills prophetic of returning spring.

From the embassadors at Rabbah-Ammon
The news had come, that well had sped their
    mission;
And that the wintry storms now only hindered
Their homeward journey, with the priceless trophy
Their diplomatic skill at length had won.

Hence when such calmer, brighter days had
  come,
As summon back from sunnier climes the birds
That through the wintry months are self-exiled,
There dawned a vision on expectant eyes,
That far outrivalled all the brilliancy
Of pluméd songsters in returning flight :
Within the palace gate, in triumph led,
Came Naamah, with charms that worthily graced
The affianced bride of Israel's mighty king.

But that which others hailed with glad acclaim,
Had, in anticipation, brought no joy
Or triumph to the heart of Solomon.
The unforgotten words of Sulamith
Had filled him with disquiet unallayed,
And started ponderings that would not cease
To urge replies to questions answerless.
With him the bound from life's simplicity
Of plans and purposes and innocent joys,
And freely chosen objects of his love,
To utter contrasts found in royalty,—
Its artificial life and luxury,
And manifold restraints that leave to kings

Far narrower liberties, in things that lie
The nearest to their hearts, than are enjoyed
By even the lowliest subjects of their realms,—
This change, so utter and so unforeseen,
Had more than tasked his mighty intellect,
Which failed to grasp the fateful consequence
Of those relationships by him unsought,
Through which an alien custom of his time,
Unhappily engrafted on his reign,
Had linked him with the women of his court.

What dread susceptibilities may sleep
In human hearts, inactive potencies,
Like garnered seed, that fertile, favoring soil
And nurturing warmth and moisture yet shall bring
To germination, growth and fruitfulness!
Of Solomon, the frank and blameless youth,
Smitten with love of wisdom, lifted high
By his ennobling aims above the lures
Of soul-debasing sensuality,
Sage, poet, lover of his brother man,
Humble and reverent worshiper of God—
None would have dreamed—until the testing change
Through which he passed its sad disclosure made—

That in his nature there were hidden germs,
Which all too readily would yield response
To reeking soil and sultry atmosphere,
That bring to tropical luxuriance
Sin's deadly poison-flowers in courts of kings.

Yet for a time he had but vaguely felt
The force of new surroundings, and his love
Still so inwrapt him with its sacredness,
That, as a coat of mail, it shielded him
From all the flying shafts of beaming eyes,
Which oftentimes assailed, with purposed aim,
The well-suspected weakness of his heart.

The subtle influence insensibly
Touched and discolored feelings hitherto
As brightly clear as drops of morning dew.
Only the eye that tries the heart and reins
Could note the slowly gathering, thickening film,
That in the end would darken all his soul.
His daily interviews with Sulamith
With much of early sweetness still were fraught,
And yet to him they brought a nameless pain,
A sense of something higher, holier

In her than aught to which he could attain ;
And when, with daring wing, she soared to heights
Glowing with splendors of unsetting suns,—
He too a sharer in her noble thoughts,
At least for golden moments,—even then,
He felt as they who dwell in valleys deep
That lie around a lofty mountain's base,
When on its topmost peak at last they stand,
And find—in greater nearness to the skies,
In high uplifting from a lowlier sphere
Of often murky, miasmatic air,
Only, alas, with strange uneasiness,
With heaving lungs, and throbbings of the heart
Quickened to painfulness—that all too pure,
Etherial, tenuous and coldly keen,
Are these free breezes of the mountain heights,
For such as they whose homes are in the vale.

Still, though his wings were drooping, for
    awhile
He fondly held his high ideals fast,
And little heed would give to grosser baits
With which the Tempter sought to snare his soul.
But evil, that had marked him for its prey,

9

Found other avenues than those of sense
Through which to reach the citadel within.
It was not for forbidden fruit he longed,
But for the unrestricted liberty
To do his kingly pleasure, hindered not
By frowning wall or flaming cherubim,
Which seemed to cross or guard the very paths
That else had led him to a chosen goal.

His pledge to Sulamith was not recalled
By any waning feeling of his heart;
But to his mind the troubling fear had come
That its fulfillment and the realm's advantage
Might prove irreconcilable : And when
The near approach of Naamah was announced,
The tidings brought to him a chafing sense,
Till then unfelt, of that exclusive bond
Which—not abjured—would make a mockery
Of this already stipulated marriage
That must in form alone be ratified.

Never had Solomon felt such pressing need
Of wisdom greater than his matchless own,
Wherewith to solve the problem which he knew

Involved his peace, perchance his destiny.
Alas, he failed to ask of him who gives
Freely to them who ask, upbraiding not;
And, worst of all, he failed in purpose high,
Come what might come, to let the right decide.
Weak compromise, or plausible excuse
For mere postponement of the evil day,—
These were his sole resort; yet all the while,
He held his pledge inviolate, his heart
Still thrilled at every thought of Sulamith.

Such was the monarch's vexed, unstable mood,
His vacillation and perplexity,
That cast their shadows, so inopportune,
Over his countenance, when now had come
The time that he must stand in Naamah's presence,
With greetings due a princess and a bride.
Alike in vain his struggles to repress
The embarrassed feeling or its visible trace,
Until before him swept the dazzling vision,
Exceeding far the praises he had heard,
Incredulous, of her surpassing charms.
As mists are scattered by the rising sun,
And all the dimness and the dreariness

Melt into mellow radiance suddenly,
So, at the brightness of that vision, fled
The gloom that darkened Solomon's heart and brow.

And who shall blame him? Beauty evermore
Must work its charm upon both sense and soul,
Nor waits for sufferance of will or conscience.
With no more guilt than in the admiring gaze
When it is drawn to nature's loveliness
Of earth or air, the landscape verdurous,
Birds, flowers, woods, mountains and the shimmering
     seas ;
Cloud-fleets that lie becalmed on azure skies,
Or float, with keels of gold, upon the floods
Of sunset radiance—as sinlessly
Are manly hearts to woman's beauty won.

The form that met the king's entrancèd gaze
Was not of queen-like stature.  On her face
Was nothing of that pure and kindling light
Of spiritual grace, which sometimes made
The face of Sulamith to shine as might
A happy, sinless angel's.  Different,
In what was visible and what unseen,

Her type of womanhood from that prevailing
Among the dark-haired maids of Israel :
Her hair was golden, and in lustre matched
The circlet of inwoven gems and pearls
That half restrained the freedom of its flow
And kept her white brow bare. Her oval face,
Of faultless feature and transparent fairness,
Made revelation of her flitting thoughts
And changeful moods, by ever answering flush
And fading of the roses on her cheeks.

Their crimson spread and deepened consciously
Under the brightening glances of the king;
And then to his her dark blue eyes were raised,
Half timidly and half appealingly,
And from them soon the light of gladness shone,
And, more than words, bespoke her recognition
Of all that she had ever hoped or dreamed
Of manly beauty and of kindly welcome
In him to whom she came a plighted bride.
The smile that played upon her lovely lips,
Her attitude of childlike eagerness,
Of happy, confident expectancy,—
All touchingly and winningly expressed

To Solomon her pleasure to be his,
The full and glad abandonment with which
She gave herself to him, and doubted not
His readiness to prize the proffered gift.

Alas, for Sulamith, and sadder far
For him whose strength before it weakness proved,—
Something in Naamah, consummate art,
Or still more formidable artlessness
That marked her as the unsophisticated child
Of nature's self, of earth the earthliest,
Yet of its finest elements compound,
And with its most seductive graces dowered—
Something in her, or rather all she was,
And much that she was not, effectively
Wrought the ensnarement of the yielding king.

Of Solomon's two-fold nature, hitherto
That which was noblest was the crowning part.
Sheltered and nurtured, growing with his growth
And strengthening with his strength, it only waned
And languished in ungenial royalty.
And sooner would the vigor of his soul,
The dominance of truth and purity
Have felt the withering blight, the weakening strain,

But for the counteracting potency
Of his deep, deathless love for Sulamith.


But now the lower self in Solomon—
Lower, yet not intrinsically base,
Or in its rightful place subordinate
To be contemned—had risen, fully armed,
Against its higher, lordlier counterpart,
In hot revolt, impetuous, resolute
To seize the sceptre and to wear the crown.


Too long within that palace-paradise
The glozing tempter had already dwelt,
Though not in serpent shape repulsive grown;
And now an incarnation he had won
Of blended loveliness and guilelessness—
Or so in seeming—that an angel's face
Might fitly wear. The siren voice that calls
The evil good, and makes it so appear,
That fatally persuades to sin and doom,
Spoke to the weakened heart of Solomon
Through tender glances of the love-lit eyes,
And smiles of winsome sweetness on the lips
Of Naamah, his beauteous heathen-bride.

In feeling, half in purpose, Solomon
Had fallen, but not yet in overt act
Of faithlessness to her, to whom was pledged
So sacredly his undivided love.
Apart from Naamah he still could rise,
Above his felt debasement, to the height
Of all his nature's former loftiness;
Then over him would sweep resistlessly
A passionate longing after Sulamith;
And, in his heart of hearts, he deeply knew
That nothing worthy in his life would live,
If he should lose her wholly, hopelessly.
In these his better moods, that rarer came
As time passed on, he sought impulsively
Her presence unto whom his soul was drawn,
As heaves the ocean toward attracting heaven.
And, for awhile, the swift and blissful hours
Of fond communings were but little marred
With painful prescience or disturbing doubt.
They came, indeed, unbidden to the heart
Of Sulamith, but always so unwelcomed,
So resolutely at the threshold fought,
They early took their flight, and left to her
An ever dwindling space of blessedness.

## XII.

## TROUBLED DREAMS.

THE brooding dove of peace, that long had dwelt
    Within the sheltering breast of Sulamith,
      Now timid grown, with wildly fluttering wing
Its home deserted ; but still hovered near,
Reluctant to depart for gathering storms,
That might compel its unreturning flight
From nesting place so sweet.

          As days dragged on,
And nights of sleeplessness or troubled dreams,
Her conflict with assailing doubts and fears
Incessant raged.  At times her mighty love,
All-conquering, routed from the battle field—
Her riven heart—these ever gathering foes.
But darker days would come, when gloom prevailed,
Misgivings triumphed, confidence was slain,
And even hope had fled.

Now rumor's tongue
Was more than ever busy with the name
And fame of Solomon; and to the ears
Of Sulamith were wafted troubling tales
Of Naamah, the Ammonitess fair,
And how her wondrous, winning loveliness
Had seemed to touch the king, as none before,
Save only Sulamith, had ever done.
And there were whisperers who brought to her
Hints of his preference manifestly shown,
Of smiles and glances, too significant,
Which had been seen to pass between the twain;
And even of stolen visits to her rooms,
Noted by envious eyes.

Though Sulamith
Would never seem to heed such idle tales—
For such she held them—still, within her heart,
They lodged and lived and bred, against her will,
A brood of turbulent and bitter thoughts;
And when day after day had passed and yet
The king came not, as daily hitherto,—
Save as his absence hindered,—he had done,
Resentment and distrust together grew.

But soon the refluent tides of tenderness
Would rise again, and all her soul would yearn
For his forgiveness, blaming but herself.

Once, when such softened mood had come to her,
With strange and troubled visions of the night—
Projection of her latest waking thought
Into the mystic, mazy realm of sleep,—
The feeling lingered through succeeding days,
And so upon her vivid fancy wrought,
That she would fain have given it expression
In tuneful song or music of her viol,
But that she would not share its sacredness
With idle or with curious listeners;
And, hence, the tender memory, the stream
Of stirred emotion and of troubled thought,
Flowed from her hand, in silent tracery
Upon her tablet, even as if it sought
Thereby to find its way to sister hearts,
Which with her own might beat in sympathy.

### SULAMITH'S DREAM.

Drowsiness over my senses crept,
But oh, it was not my heart that slept:
In vision or in reality
He whom it loves drew near to me;
He stood and knocked at my bolted door,
As he oft had stood and knocked before.
My soul's deep tenderness was stirred,
Whilst the music of his voice I heard
  Again and again,
  With this sad refrain,
Pleading for entrance—but in vain.

"I am pining, oh, sister-spouse, for thee.
Open, my dove undefiled, to me!
  I have waited until
  With night-dews chill
My locks are wet; and I wait, wait still."

Deep slumber had all my powers enthralled,
Yet I woke when my belovèd called;
But the words with which my lips replied
The love of my yearning heart belied;
For I lightly said or seemed to say,

In mocking excuse for my delay :
"My robe I have laid aside with care,
My feet for the night are bathed and bare ;
    Sleep so seals my eyes,
    That I cannot rise
Till the birds shall sing to the purpling skies.''

He humbly pleads who might well command,
From royal throne and with sceptred hand,
That hand—a suppliant's now—I see,
Through the door's opening, stretched toward me.
Not long does it mutely plead in vain ;
Love's swelling tide rises high amain,
And it bears me on its mighty flow.
(But waking or sleeping, who could know?)
From my flowing hair and finger tips
The sweetness of myrrh and aloes drips,
As my eager hands undo the door ;
But ah, on its threshold waits no more,
    In the dim starlight
    Of the chill, damp night,
My only belovèd, my soul's delight.

He had turned away, for alas, too long

Had my idle dalliance done him wrong.
I saw a shadowy form that fled,
And after it, waking or sleeping, sped.
Swift as a roe's, my unsandaled feet
Threaded the narrow and flinty street,
Till the form I followed in my flight
Seemed only a phantom of the night;
  And to my wild cry
  There came no reply
Through the gloom that deepened on earth and sky.

My strength both of soul and of limbs gave way,
I fell, and prone on the cold ground lay.
Soon the watchmen's torches over me flared,
Their pitiless eyes upon me glared;
And they fiercely spurned me with their feet,
As they might some vile thing of the street.
I swooned, from the mortal dread and shame,
And all was a blank till morning came.
Then, at the opening of my eyes,
With mingled wonder and surprise
And tearful joy, did I recognize,
Above my softly pillowed head,
The silken canopy of my bed;

And saw, in the blending light and shade,
That fitfully through my chamber played,
On the carvèd ceiling and the floor,
All that I oft had noted before;
And knew things were not what they seemed,
That the night's strange horrors were but dreamed!
No bruises upon my flesh were found,
But my heart still bleeds with an inward wound,
  And thrills with pain,
  That again and again—
Though but in a dream—my love plead in vain.

Oh, Jerusalem's daughters, if it be
That you my belovèd one shall see,
Speak not of the dream my fancy wove,
But say I am sad and sick of love.

## XIII.

## PARADISE LOST.

IKE hapless barque within the whirlpool's
rim,
Unstemmed the circling current's eddying
flow,
The downward swirl that to the vortex bears,
So was it with the passion-driven king.

Like witless moth of shining, silken wing,
Enamored with the taper's fatal blaze,
Still to the bright allurement nearer drawn,
And in its fierce enfoldings soon to die,
So was it with this wisest of the wise—
His folly and its fruit of destiny.

How are the mighty fallen ! Prostrate lie
Honor and faithfulness and purity.
Yet in his heart, not heedless of its guilt,

Still lived and reigned his love for Sulamith ;
And when, from passion and illusion free,
His nobler self brief mastery regained,
Such impulse stirred within him restlessly
As drove him to her side.

                Could it have been
That what was in his vivid consciousness
Was written on his face? Did broken vows,
A sense of tarnished honor and untruth,
His wrongfulness of heart and life—as yet
Not otherwise disclosed—signal their shame
Through something of its former brightness fled?

When Sulamith, from troubled musings roused,
First recognized the presence of the king,
Over her countenance, like sunrise, spread
The tender light of love. Her glad surprise
Her happy welcome told. But as her eyes—
Through which her very soul looked searchingly,
As though it fain would fathom what it deemed
Love's soundless depths in his—still rested on him,
Some shadow as of intercepting cloud,
Some disappointing change that met her gaze,
Brought swift eclipse to all her beaming joy.

10

Backward she shrank and partly turned away.
The crimson bloom forsook her paling cheek,
The love-light vanished and her features wore—
Through sudden transformation—such a look,
So fraught with deadly pain, yet fixed and frozen,
And stamped with resolution firm and high,
That Solomon, who had been drawing near
With eager face and with extended arms,
Made instant pause, and to his brow there shot
A flush of anger or of wounded pride
Or of insulted love, as it might be
With one who for caresses looked and longed,
But in their stead received a stinging blow.

Then to the tumult of her soul there came
The recollection that, whatever else
He was or was not unto her, yet he
Was still the Lord's anointed and her king :
Hence, with due reverence for the majesty,
That in its changeless sacredness remained,
Though truth were lost and honor's lustre dimmed,
She bowed before him, but with veiléd eyes,
And only as a stranger-subject might,
In meek obeisance, waiting on his will.

Then spake the king when, after silence brief,
The storm of passion in his breast was lulled :

"Too plainly I perceive, oh, Sulamith,
That thou hast knowledge more than seemeth meet
Or for thy peace or good.  Birds of the air
Bear unto thee, upon their mischievous wings,
Even secrets of the chamber whispered low.
Some raven croaking evil of the king,
Who holds thee dearest, thou hast surely heard :
But know, belovéd, judgment often errs
In rash condemning of the one accused,
Who on his own behalf hath answered not.
The assailant's cause, first plead, seems ever right
Till the assailed doth come and searcheth him.

" Departure from the tenor of my pledge
And purpose of my heart to be but thine,
Save as to empty name, and form of marriage,
I needs must own.  But when that pledge was given,
I knew not that the inevitable stress
Of those conditions, which I vainly dreamed
Were wholly at my royal disposition,
Would sway my sceptre, would usurp my throne.

And hold me vassal to its sovereignty
Even in that against which, most of all,
My wish and will alike strove helplessly.
So much, I own, my plighted word has failed;
But none beside thee shares, or ever can,
In that sole love which, with my heart, my life,
Myself, my throne, my all, I give to thee.


"I hold such marriage state most excellent
As God did first ordain in Paradise,
Wherein the twain, one man, one woman meet,
Forsaking others all, cleave each to each,
And so become one flesh.  For joy of wedlock,
Its peace and good, and for all human weal,
God's plan for Eden for the world were best.
Yet, in its fallen state, He hath not held
With rigor to that primal Eden law.
Even holy patriarchs from it turned aside
For other wives than one, nor were condemned.
And shall my royal father's memory
The less be honored, that, in this estate
Of marriage multifold, he lived and died,
Of men approved and by Jehovah loved?
I follow in the brightened path he trod,

Guiltless, save in my broken pledge to thee.
For this, thy clemency I humbly crave.
Grant to my smitten heart this healing balm,
And from the wreck of thy lost confidence,
Thus shattered on the shoals of unknown seas,
Made skillful by experience early gained
From lessons of perplexity and pain,
These hands a stauncher structure shall erect,
In which thy soul may dwell, without a fear
Of damage to be wrought by further change."

"Speak one forgiving word. Oh, lift again
The brightness of those downcast eyes on me.
Tell me the day for which my soul has longed
And watched, as they who through a dreary night
Watch for the morning, even now is near,
When thy sweet promise to be wholly mine
Shall be fulfilled. Then hear my kingly oath:
Within my heart and ever at my side,
Upon my throne thy place supreme shall be.
The daughters all shall bless thee, and the queens
And concubines shall praise thee. Only thou,
Their queen and mine, shalt honored mother be
Of him who, after me, shall sit upon

The throne of David, and from whom shall spring
The illustrious line of Israel's mighty kings,
Till He at last shall come, the Promised One,
Who over all the conquered world shall reign."

The monarch's words, as never in the past,
Rang hollow in the ears of Sulamith.
A sudden change within her had been wrought,
That made his wisdom seem no longer wise;
And all the feeling of his fervid speech
Failed to awake an echo in her heart.
Nor had the faithful teaching of her sire
Left her unarmed against the sophistry
With which the king essayed to set aside
God's marriage law for Eden and the world—
Never repealed, nor ever weaker grown;
Its penalties exacted,—at the hands
Of best and greatest who against it sinned,—
In broken peace of homes, in broods of crimes
And woes that from its violation sprang;
Its woman-victims always first and last
And chief of sufferers.  Such was the thought
That flashed like lightning through her mind, and slew
The error of his speech.

Indignantly,
And shamed as for herself, she also heard
Him, she had manliest deemed, confess himself
Too weak to keep his word inviolate
Against the tyranny of usages
To Israel brought from heathen courts and kings;
And only that her grieved but deathless love
And rising pity plead on his behalf,
She would have answered him with words of scorn.

A moment's silence, while her struggling will
Sought mastery of the stormy turbulence
And chaos of her sorely stricken heart;
Then, with slow utterance, as of one who weighs
Each word, as if its freight were life or death,
She spoke her low, sad answer to the king:

"Thou say'st thy vow is broken. I am thus
Absolved of mine; but oh, I find it naught
But vain and bitter sorrow to be free;
And still, my heart is holden with dear bonds
Not even death shall break.

"In Lebanon
A shepherd youth was mine. I only his.

In this our sole and mutual possession
Each of the other, we were well content,
With an abounding blessedness to which
The riches of a world could add no more.
But all too soon there came a fateful day
When he departed. Weary months passed by,
Yet neither he nor tidings of him came.
But when, at length, the hope of his return,
On which my soul had fed as for its life,
Had dwindled till it seemed the meager crust,
The last poor morsel of the failing hoard,
Which when the famine-stricken one should eat,
He would but wait to die,—then came to me
One who declared himself my lost one found.
All that he seemed confirmed the welcome claim
To my fond heart, which what it wished believed,
And so repelled misgivings, until now,
That from its fortressed door they, vanquished, fled.

"Alas, the very lips, from which my soul
Drank in the sweet deception, speak the words
That break its spell forever. Now I know
That he, the crownéd king of Israel,
Who yields—for customs greater than his throne,

And stronger than his might—his liberty
To keep his sacred word to her whose all
Was staked upon its truth and steadfastness,
Is wholly other than my loved and lost.
Hence nothing else is left for Sulamith—
Her grievous error known—but to lament
Her shepherd dead! Her virgin widowhood
Would illy sort with mirth of palace halls,
And must no longer cast its shadow here.
One only boon she craves ; henceforth to dwell
With her sad memories in the shadowed haunts
Of cedared Lebanon, her fitting home.''

More than the pathos of the maiden's words,
Its veiléd imputation touched the king—
A keen-edged sword which, through all subterfuge,
His quickened conscience pierced, and roused his wrath
Against himself, to such intensity
That its hot lightnings flashed in petulant words ;
And, in his swift reply to Sulamith,
He hinted of her duty to obey
His royal mandates, and reminded her
That even the love with which he honored her
Worked no absolving of her loyalty ;

And that, wherein his gentleness had failed,
His sovereign power might forcefully compel.


With patient meekness yet with dignity,
Deep grief and pity blending in her tones,
Thus Sulamith his tide of passion stemmed :


"Oh, Solomon, my king !—that such thou art,
Most gladly would I own, if this poor heart
And gladness had not parted.—Humbly, then,
I own thee king ; but only such, to me,
Henceforth, save in my treasured memories
Of what is past and gone beyond recall.
So well I know thy wisdom and, far more,
The kindness of thy great and kingly heart,
I cannot fear thy power. No power hast thou
That ever can avail to make of me—
Weak and defenceless as I surely am,
Were I not girdled with Almighty arms—
One of the multitude thou callest wives.
At most thou can'st but slay me, if thou wilt ;
But death has lost its terror, since from life
Its trusted love and blessedness have fled.
Oh, sweet, methinks, the mortal blow would be,

If dealt by thy dear hand.  Yes, I can die,
As Jeptha's virgin daughter proudly died ;
As true, tried hearts have often welcomed death ;
But cannot live, oh king, for even thee,
A life my soul would loathe and count its shame."

As to her lofty words the baffled king
Gave heed, his anger died away.  Remorse
And shame of self reigned only in its room.
The maiden, marble pale and statue-like,
With drooped and tearless eyes, but look of pain
Unutterable, far above him seemed
To tower in regal, stainless purity ;
And all the glory of great Solomon
Dwindled and groveled at her queenly feet.
Nor did he dare to lay his soiléd hand
Upon her garment's hem.  Never before,
Within him stirred such yearning for her love,
As now, when with a pang like death, he felt
That, prized by him the most, she was to him
Most lost—forever lost !  It was with him
As it might be with one who saw, at last,
A saintly spirit, linked awhile to his
By earthly love alone, and beautiful

In all the grace of ripened holiness,
Pluming its full-fledged wings for heavenward flight,
Which he can only follow with his gaze
Of wistful longing, sadly, hopelessly!

\* \* \* \* \* \* \* \* \*

One rose the less on Sharon's blooming plain;
One leaf dropped noiseless from the foliage
That forms a forest's verdant canopy;
One star that shines no longer from a sky
Crowded with constellations numberless,
And nebulous mazes woven of bright worlds;—
Plucked rose, leaf fallen, veiled or vanished star,
Unmissed of common eyes; so, missed scarce more,—
Save by the humbled, troubled, heart-sick king,—
Passed silently from out the palace halls,
And all the brilliant throngs that brightened them,
Sad, desolate, triumphant Sulamith.

Around the vine-clad slopes of Lebanon
The mists are gathering, and, lo! they hide
The stately form on which our charmèd eyes
Have lingered long, the form of beauty rare,
That shrined a soul more rarely beautiful—
A soul whose might of love was held in thrall

By the surpassing might of loyalty
To God and duty, to the truth and right
And sacred claim of woman's purity.

What acts she further did, what other wars
She warred with her fond heart, which ever yearned
In deathless love and pity over him,
The captive king, who sold his nobleness
For Esau's portion served in royal state,
And lost a treasure that outweighed the world ;
What paths of usefulness she meekly trod,
So gaining meetness for that higher sphere
Where faithfulness shall wear its rightful crown ;
And how such winning grace her life illumed
As many a wanderer lured from devious ways,
To follow where her upward footprints led ;
And how her unextinguished memory
Wrought with the recreant king, and held him back
From deeper plunges into fatal depths,
And proved at last the clue wherewith he found
A homeward way, through wildering labyrinths,
To his forsaken God, then gave to him—
When from his vileness purged—the elements
From which, with heavenly help, his guided hand

That wondrous poem penned, which celebrates
The beauty, blessedness and sanctity
Alike of earthly and of heavenly love :—
All these, and what beside, that Sulamith
Did first and last, behold, are they not written
By the Recording Angel in the book
Which shall be opened on that Day of days,
The light of which shall show how many a name,
Of men forgotten, leads the shining lists
Of martyr-spirits, unto whom the world,
That is not worthy of them, owes its best ?

# Night.

Not lost is all the glory of the light
When day is ended, and the chariot
Of its illustrious king has downward rolled,
Below the far horizon's purple rim.
Long lingers, on the westward slope, the glow
Caught from its burning wheels.  O'er land and sea
The veil of twilight, softly luminous,
To nature's features lends a grace unknown
Beneath the glaring brightness of the day;
And, as the shadows deepen, stars steal out,
And grow in radiance and multiply,
Until they glitter from the darkened sky
Like jewels gleaming on the sable brow
Of Ethiopian queen.  The silvery moon
Shines in her crescent beauty, chastely cold;
Or with her full-orbed splendor floods the world;
Or, through the moonless air the meteor sweeps,
With self-consuming blaze that pales the stars;
Or comet-visitants, from realms remote,
With trains magnificent that mark their state,

159

Speed their erratic flight past wondering worlds ;
Or the aurora, born amid the floes
Of polar seas, flames on the northern sky,
And darts its rose-tinged streaks from north to south,
Or, with swift spreading of its crimson waves,
Suffuses all the heavens and snow-clad earth :—
Thus ofttimes reigns the brilliance of the night,
From fading twilight until glimmering dawn.

# XIV.

## VANITY OF VANITIES.

FOR Solomon the brief bright day of love
And innocence was past.  And now the night
Of evil dominating over good
Had its beginnings, which were doomed to grow
Till they should deepen into midnight gloom.

But long with him it seemed, as in the lands
Far northward, when, behind their icy cliffs,
The sun has scarcely more than disappeared,
And, as in flight suspended, from below
The gleaming steep illumes the western sky;
So making twilight, such as untaught eyes
Might easily mistake for shadowed day.

The brightness of his mighty intellect
Had suffered no eclipse.  His eye, undimmed,
Pierced to the hidden substances of things,

11

And made discrimination, clear and keen,
Between the chaff and wheat, the dross and gold.
God's gift of wisdom still was unrevoked,
And with his culture grew, till it excelled
Even that by Egypt treasured and the East,
Through ages grown.  Phrases proverbial,
Compact and terse, true wisdom's garnered seed
Whose deathless germs are now wide-branching trees,
On fruits of which when men or nations feed
They grow to greatness,—thousands such as these
By him were wrought, and thousands more of songs
Flowed from his pen.  Of trees he also spake,
From Lebanon's cedar to the hyssop plant
That draws its humbler growth from crevices
Of moldering, moss-grown walls ; and of all beasts
And birds and fishes, and of creeping things.
A pioneer of science far renowned !
Around him gathered peoples of all lands,
Attracted by his wisdom's widening fame ;
And kings and queens made weary pilgrimage
To see and hear this marvel of their kind.

　　No idle dreamer even of great dreams,
Nor fruitless theorist was Solomon.

His high conceptions wrought effectively
In works of art or use beneficent,
That were the pride of Israel and drew
The world's admiring gaze.  Of these first, chief,
The glorious Temple—from foundation stones
To golden pinnacles that skyward flamed—
In sacred silence magic-like arose,
A monument of richest, brightest, best,
To speak of God transcendent over all.
Then Ophel's brow received its palace-crown ;
Then massive Millo, and the stately tower
Of David's House, hung round with brazen shields,
All shields of mighty men.  The city wall
Rose to defiant height, and through the land,
On every route of commerce or where foes
Might access find, were frowning fortresses—
On the Damascus road in Lebanon,
Hard by the summer-palace beautiful
With pillared porches, all of cedar wrought ;
Hazon that threatening towered above Merom ;
Baalath, and Beth-Horon's guarded pass,
To stem invasion pouring from the sea.
And, quickened into life by growing thrift
And enterprise, such cities had their birth

As Tadmor, in the oasis of palms,
Far out upon the Desert's arid way
Through which the trade of Egypt northward flowed,
Till intercepted by this new-made mart
That stood and flourished for a thousand years.
Orchards and vineyards; parks with planted trees
For fruit and beauty and delicious shade;
And fountains which, with never-ceasing flow,
Kept moist and cool what else were torrid air;
Great aqueducts that poured unfailing streams
Into vast reservoirs of masonry,
That lapsing ages leave unworn,—all these
Were Solomon's embodied thoughts, and proofs
That he was no enervate Sybarite,
But greatly practical as greatly wise.

Staunch merchant ships at Ezion Geber built
By skilled Phenician workmen, stoutly manned
By sailors reared in Dan and Zebulon,
Made daring voyages to far-off lands,—
To Tarshish for its precious metals famed,
To Ophir where was mined the finest gold,
To mouths of Indus rich in sandal wood,
Even to Afrique coasts whence novel freights

Of ivory, ebony and apes were brought ;
And when, each third year from their setting sail,
The strained and shattered but enduring craft
Returned, full-laden, stately caravans
Their costly cargoes wearily conveyed
Through gathering crowds to ceaseless wonder stirred.
So did these ever widening, deepening streams
Of commerce flow and pour their shining floods,
That gold grew plentiful as scattered stones
Upon the city street, and silver ceased
To be accounted of in Israel.

The culminating glory of the land,
As promised, now was reached.   Its boundaries
Unto Orontes stretched from the Red Sea,
And from the western waves to where yet flows
Euphrates, with its proud, sad memories
Of Eden-flowers that on its banks once bloomed.

Thus wide the realm which David's conquests
          gave
To Solomon.   And, through its length and breadth,
Under his sway benign and merciful,
Yet strong to cope with evil, Israel

And Judah dwelt in concord undisturbed ;
And every man was safe beneath the vine
And fig tree that embowered his happy home.
His power deliverance brought to the oppressed,
And to the poor and needy swift relief ;
The wronged, who had no helper, he redeemed
From violence, and precious in his sight
Was ever held the blood of innocence.

Two nameless women once before him came,
Bringing an infant boy, of which each claimed
To be the mother.　Each her story told,
Equally positive and equally
Devoid of proof.　"A sword !" the monarch cried ;
And forthwith flashed before the eyes of all
The unsheathed weapon.　Then King Solomon
His sentence curtly gave : The headsman's sword
Should equitably cleave the child in twain,
And to each claimant duly give her half.
One, with pale face and look of agony,
As though the glittering blade had pierced her heart,
Shrieked out, "Not so !　In no wise slay the child,
Let it be hers."　But, to the king's decree,
The other promptly signified assent.

And unto her whose yearning motherhood
Had leapt to save her little one from death,
Though from her bosom reft, the child was given.

Thus did the wondrous wisdom of the king
Shed piercing light on depths of hidden wrong,
That killed its roots ere from them rankly sprang
The noxious growth of violence and crime.
So human life well guarded, nurtured well,
Had matchless, marvelous development.
Judah and Israel were many, even as sand
On the sea shore for multitude, eating
And drinking merrily, day by day;
And to the land had come its golden age—
Its first and last, of two-score fleeting years.

But, ah, in him to whose illustrious reign,
Of wisdom, peacefulness, benignity,
The age's glory, under God, was due,
The gold that gave it lustre had been dimmed,
And changed the most fine gold—his honor, truth
And purposed purity of heart and life.
But still so slightly or so slowly wrought
The subtle tarnishing, that common eyes

Were dazzled, blinded long; and not a breath
Of popular dispraise detracted aught
From the transcendent splendor of his fame.

One sole and burdening sense of wrongfulness
Upon the spirit of the monarch weighed.
It was not an accusing consciousness
Of vassalage to lusts, unworthy held
Of man's supremacy above the brute;
For not as yet his self-asserting soul
Had fully owned so gross a mastery.
Nor was it that, in part from policy,
In part from personal preference, he had made
Fair Naamah his bride, and not alone
In empty form and name.  For not a doubt
Disturbed his conscience of the lawfulness
Of this, or other added marriages,
Which he might make, in strict conformity
To precedents by him deemed questionless.

The self-abasing, torturing memory
That rankling dwelt within him night and day,
Was of his kingly word to Sulamith
Trodden so shamefully beneath his feet,

In his mad haste to reach the tempting fruit
That proved but ashes to his sickened taste.
And ever to his soul her image shone
In fadeless, stainless beauty, as a star
Shines on the far sky, inaccessible.
And oft he lashed, with bitter, burning scorn,
His wretched folly that, for nothingness,
Had forfeited a prize which to his heart
Was more than all the grandeur and renown
Of Israel's glorious kingdom or a world's !

The childlike loveliness of Naamah,
Her graceful form and gleaming, golden hair,
And face with gladness often lit, and yet
At times half shadowed with a wistfulness
That touched all hearts with its appealing grace,
Had much of fascination for the king ;
And, but that his one quenchless passion swayed
His heart exclusively, it might at last
Have wrought in him the manly tenderness
That often answers well for manly love.
Her voiceless eloquence of looks and smiles
Made large amends for scantiness of speech ;
And long it seemed enough for Solomon,

That sense of beauty, heart and sight were charmed,
Though for his ear her voice no thrilling spell
Of music wrought ; nor flash of intellect,
Nor glowing thought responsive matched the light
And warmth which had their dwelling place in him.

It was as if were paired a sea's expanse
Of mighty pulsing tides and fathomless,
And an adjacent pool, of grassy marge,
Reflecting from the brightness of its face
The glories of the ever changing sky ;
Rippled and dimpled by the sportive breeze,
But by the stormy winds, that leave unstirred
The vast sea-depths, its shallowness exposed ;
Its waters to the bottom lightly swept ;
So laying bare, to vex the gazer's eye,
The unsightly slime and mire that lay concealed
Beneath the glassy sheen, through sunny hours.

Long lingered the illusion, yet too soon
For peace of Solomon the tempest came ;
And all the surface brightness, which had cheered
At times his gloom and loneliness of soul,
Fled from the darkening face of Naamah.

From her now livid lips a stream of words,
In shrillest discords, freely, fiercely flowed.
The shallows of her soul were broken up,
And, to the shocked, bewildered king, were bared
The unsuspected filth and odiousness
Of heathen grossness, littleness and spite
Her beauty's brightness until then had veiled.

The burst of rage which, like a bitter blast,
Blighted the bloom and beauty of her face,
And spoiled its fascination for the king,
Had weighty cause : Her love for Solomon
Had proved of passionate intensity,
Ere since her pulses fluttered at the sight
Of his majestic form, his smile benign
Of welcome that dispelled her maiden fears,
When through his palace-gate she first had passed,
A stranger-bride ; and, in her narrow heart—
With this one dominating sentiment
Entwined, identified—the purpose grew
To win and keep the highest place in his,
To be his wife of wives, his queen of queens ;
Nor, since the noiseless flight of Sulamith,
Had aught of serious hindrance come between

Her womanly ambition and its aim.
The king had seemed to care for none beside;
And blissful motherhood had early crowned
Her tenderest wish, and sweet assurance given
Of full fruition to her proudest hope.

The cloud which, even at the noontide hour
Of her elation, darkened all her sky,
Was from the advent, loudly heralded,
Of Pharaoh's daughter, who had been espoused
To Solomon, and so become the bond
Which in a close alliance now should hold
The might of Egypt and of Israel.
With royal equipage and stateliness,
That totally eclipsed the pageantries
Of all her predecessors, she had come,
Greeted with welcoming festivities
That testified the pleasure of the king.

The disenchanting wrath of Naamah—
For her ill-timed—had snapt the fragile bond,
Dissolved the thralling spell, wherewith her charms
First strongly drew, then held him long her own.
Hence when his now no longer dazzled eyes

Gazed on the Egyptian's regal form and mien,
Her darkly brilliant beauty—star-lit night!—
Her languid eyes, magnetic with the power
Of slumbering passion,—his unanchored heart
Drifted once more, unhindered, on the tides
Which, at the new attraction, swelled and flowed.

So had it come to pass that Naamah
Thus self-deposed from her supremacy—
This statelier daughter of a mightier king,
Dowered with a city's site, which Pharaoh,
Her royal sire had wrested from the hands
Of its Phenician habitants, became
Chiefest among the wives of Solomon;
And, as a crownèd queen, she shared alike
His grandeur and his royal eminence.

But, from her exaltation, speedily,
A great, and in the end, disastrous change
Passed o'er the monarchy and all the land.
The simpler usages of purer times,
Before this alien spirit now enthroned,
Gave way, and left an ever widening place
To pomp and artificiality,

And kindred vices of extravagance,
That, from the seeds of evil, earlier sown,
Now rankly grew and bore their baneful fruits.
And most, within the heart of Solomon,
What least was noble sprang to perilous strength
Under the fostering influence to which
He made surrender, won by sensuous charms,
And wrought upon by unsuspected arts,
Coupled with wilfulness too well concealed.

A deeper taint, a darker, deadlier stain
At length had touched the conscience of the king,
Through his affinity with her who came
From Egypt, most prolific of all lands
In idols and their zealous votaries.
True, outwardly, she oft had joined with him
In sacrificial rites and services
That owned the God of Israel God alone:
But all the while—long hidden from the eyes
Of Solomon, within a deep recess,
A secret chamber of her palace-home—
She daily bowed her knee before a shrine
At which the homage of her soul was paid
To a sincerely worshiped deity—

A golden Isis, woman-like in form,
With sistrum in her hand, her hornèd brow
Crowned with a wreath of sacred Lotus flowers !

    At last to Solomon, by chance, had come
Unwelcomed knowledge of the shocking truth,
That she who in his bosom slept, and sat
With him on Israel's throne, thus secretly
In adoration bent before the shrine
Of an Egyptian idol.  Grief and shame
Unutterable, swelled within his heart
At the discovery ; for not as yet
Was he disloyal, even in his thought,
To Israel's King of kings, his father's God,
In whose sole name he reigned, and ministered
As royal priest in all the services
That to His altar and His house pertained.
But, ah, the flaming zeal that once had blazed
To purge such desecrating stain, to avenge
Such insult to Jehovah and the place
His presence hallowed, brightly glowed no more—
Was but the flickering spark upon the coal
That dies and blackens in the smothering damps
Of waning faith, decaying piety.

A compromise with conscience was the most
That its enfeebled life at length secured;
A base connivance with the deadly wrong;
For still the abomination was endured,
And not a word he spake that would displease
The queen, whose blended charms and artifice
Held him no less submissively enthralled.

But though the outrage still should live and
thrive,
Yet should its loathèd presence violate
No more, thereafter, Zion's sacredness.
A stately, costly palace should be reared
On ground less holy, where, with freer range
And greater privacy, she might thenceforth
Do all her pleasure, as became a queen.

Thus, step by step, with slow but sure descent,
The king had reached a level sadly low
Compared with that from which his reign began;
And when the years, that ever swifter flew,
Had brought to him—long busied and absorbed
With vast designs that kept his soul enlarged,
And exercised its nobler faculties—

Ensuing leisure, ease and luxury,
Then, prompt to hail their opportunity,
The hovering vices that had nearer drawn,
Swooped on their destined prey, the monarch's
 heart,
So feebly guarded, so unoccupied!

He who had drank deep draughts of love's
 delight
From early Eden-fountains undefiled ;
He who had known the satisfying bliss
Of fellowship congenial, soul with soul,
Feeling and thought respondent, each to each,
And mated equally, had vainly sought
For fresh experience of such blessedness ;
And vainly dreamed that he might haply find,
In new relationships, what yet should fill
The void within him by his folly wrought.

A hollow, disappointed, restless heart
Had come to be the doom of Solomon ;
And his were soon foretokenings of a time,
Not distant, when satiety should be
The burden of that heart, the bitter end

12

Of all to which its craving and its pain
Impelled him. And not now, as in the past,
Did will or conscience longer hold in check
The animal which threatened to outgrow
The ever dwindling soul. Nor failed the plea,
Ancient and plausible and often made
For loosened rein on fleshly appetite,
In lawless search of wisdom,—"wisdom found,"
So reasoned he, "in freer, wider range
Of living, and a fuller knowledge to be gained
By closer intercourse with human kind.
Not sight alone of glowing fruits that hung
On trees forbidden, but the actual taste,
Would true acquaintance of their nature give."

And thus, with calculation shrewd and cool,
He gave his manhood's ripening and strength
To wine's exhilaration, and laid hold
On human folly, with the fond pretense
Of thereby drawing forth disclosures new,
For future furtherance of the good of man.
And all voluptuous pleasures he would prove
And accurately weigh, and unto each
Assign its proper valuation. Hence

Whatever sight of beauty charmed his eyes,
Or joy of taste or sense allured his heart,
From this—unquestioning either of the right
Or wrong—his hands were not withheld;
And, in the prosecution of his search,
Its last and worst extreme of rash adventure,
To trace the reasons recondite of things,
To know what madness and what wickedness
Oft dwell in hearts of men, and mold their lives
Into the monster shapes of crime and woe
That move to horror or that melt to tears,
He found—how little wonder that he found!—
Perverted woman's sad supremacy
Among the evil; bitterer than death
Her heart of snares and nets; her soft, fair hands
Bands irresistible that captive lead
Too willingly beguiled and ruined men.

Ah! vivisectionist of human souls,
At what a cost thy added lore is gained,
Or noblest skill or art is perfected,
To hapless victims keenly sensitive,
Who bleed and writhe in thine unfaltering hands.
Oh! cruel sharpness of the knife which lays

All bare the quivering nerve, that darts its thrills
Of mortal anguish to the conscious brain,
Or pierces to the quick of shrinking hearts
To find their deepest secrets, which, henceforth,
Assorted, labeled, have conspicuous place
In cabinets of metaphysic sage,
Or, by the hand of genius deftly wrought,
Give fascinating power and vividness
To painter's picture or to poet's dream.

But eminently hapless and undone
Is woman, dowered with rare capacities
Of pain and pleasure, woe and blessedness—
Woman, with springs unfathomed in her breast
Of tender sweetness and of matchless love,
Whenever thus unscrupulously made
Mere ministress of cold philosophy,
Or ruthless art, or—worse immeasurably—
The plaything, and the victim in the end,
Of selfish sensualist, who smiles and slays
That which in woman's life is sacredest.

The sleepless Nemesis that evermore
Implacably avenges womanhood

Thus cruelly wronged, with whips of scorpions,
Plied by his victims, scourged the offending king.
From blighted innocence its tender bloom
And beauty fled. The brightness of its joy,
Its sparkling merriment, its ringing songs,
Were darkened, silenced, by the gathering storms
Of clashing rivalries irrepressible,
That in the throngèd harem ever dwell.
And, in that sensuous atmosphere, surcharged
With stimulated passions gross and low,
The deadly crop, that sowing to the flesh
Fails not to yield, was early harvested ;
All evil fermentations swiftly wrought ;
And what was womanly sweetness turned, at last,
To wormwood on the lips of Solomon.

Unhappiest of kings ! for lo, the crown
Of his pre-eminence was now a crown
Of thorns,—keen self-accusings,—and inwreathed
With twining, hissing serpents of remorse,
That brooding memories hatched ceaselessly
Within his tortured brain.

And what to him
Were gaudy flowers that in his palace bloomed,
And breathed rank odors, as from oozy sod
And heavy, fetid air?—what were they all
To him who saw in memory's softened light
That one sweet, regal lily of the vale,
Unstained as falling snowflake—thought of God,
In fairest earthly vesture fitly clad—
For him, for him alone, but which his hand,
Made reckless by the folly of his heart,
In mad exchange for these had flung away?

A smaller soul than that of Solomon
Could not have known the utter emptiness
Which—after all this desperate endeavor,
With whatsoe'er his subject realm, or wealth
Of distant lands by commerce brought could give,
Or royal power command, to fill the void—
Left him as one who feeds upon the wind.
A nature less capacious might have found
Its narrowness replete and satisfied
With such magnificence of kingly state,
Such victories of peace, such growing power,
And widening empire, and unruffled flow

Of personal and national events
As signalized this favored monarch's reign ;
One more ignobly, grossly sensual,
In such unstinted luxury, such range
Of license limitless, even as an ox
In fenceless pasture grazing,—surfeiting
Thus brutally his animal appetite—
A brute's contentment might have well enjoyed,
Nor cherished wish or care for aught beyond.
But oh, not so with soul like Solomon's ;
For it had largeness ample as the shore
That with its sandy, shelving beach wave-worn,
Or stretch of coast, rock-bound or mountainous,
Encompasses the vastness of a sea.
And when all royal might and majesty,
All riches gathered from the land and main,
All grand achievements wrought or glories won,
Or triumphs proud of intellect or art,
Or stores of wisdom more than rubies prized,
Or sensuous joys, or beauty's witchery,
Or wine's enchantment, or the reveler's mirth,—
When all these countless rivers of delight
Had flowed into this sea, it was not full.
This mighty soul's infinitude !—oh, still

Its hollowness resounded, night and day,
With outcries of unsatisfied desire,
Plaints of a weary, satiated heart,
Sickened and hopeless, sighing evermore
Like ocean's moaning winds that drear refrain:
VANITY! VANITIES! ALL IS VANITY!

## The Hurrying Years.

As in my view, O hurrying years!
The havoc ye have wrought appears,
Mine eyes o'erflow with bitter tears.

Your robber hands, of all the grace
Of rounded form and blooming face,
Have left, alas, no lingering trace.

How fair was earth when life was new;
How green the fields, the skies how blue!
What spring flowers, gemmed with morning dew!

A magic touch the past unseals,
Its beauty and its bliss reveals;
But lo, a flash of flying wheels,—

The chariot wheels of Time, that bear
From rifled youth its treasures rare.
All gone ; naught left but age and care.

Vainly we pray, or vainly weep,
And strive our best beloved to keep;
Upon them falls the dreamless sleep.

The hero's sword has gathered rust,
The arm that wielded it is dust,
Deceived or failed his high heart's trust.

Rain on, ye tears of bitterest ruth,
For more than faded, vanished youth,—
Soiled innocence, lost God and truth!

Much still were mine, though all beside
Were from me swept, as on the tide
Of rivers swift that seaward glide,
Should faith and hope and love abide.

## XV.

## SIN AND SORROW.

THE curse that comes to him to whom the
 world,
  Whether of sense or intellect or art,
Has grown to be his all, had settled down
Upon the mind and soul of Solomon.
Even the visible beauty of the earth
And sea and sky took on a duller hue;
And nature more and more had come to be
But a dead organism, hard and cold,
From which had fled the all-pervading Soul,
That erst, with its felt immanence, had awed
And swayed him, or his deepest feelings stirred
To tenderness and tears. The face and form
Of Sulamith had faded, and no more
Brought back the vanished rapture to his dreams.
And—deepest of all woes!—as wildly far
This royal wanderer still darkly strayed

Into the paths of worldliness and sin. —
As thus unhappy, guilty Solomon
From God departed, even so did God,
In holy grief and righteousness, withdraw
Not solely from the offender's consciousness,
But from the hallowed symbols which before
Were visibly with His dread presence fraught.
Within the High Priest's vesture idly shone
Urim and Thummim, that no longer flashed
With signal lights unearthly in response
To such as asked what God would have them do :
And, from the temple's holiest recess,
Above the Ark, between the Cherubim,
The cloud that with shekinah blazed was gone.
Prophetic vision ceased.  No more by dreams,
As twice to Solomon in happier years,
When heart and ear were open to His voice,
Came faintest whisper of the will  divine.

Oh, dreary world ! oh, orphaned universe !
Oh, blankness, darkness of the infinite void !
That give not to the deepest, highest thought,
Or yield not unto agonizing prayer,
The God dethroned and lost through unbelief ;

Or who from chosen sin incorrigible
Has hid at last the brightness of His face.

Sin willfully cherished, breeding unbelief,
Was that which to the sense of Solomon,
And even to his mighty intellect,
In all its grasp immense and upward reach,
Had banished God from thought and temple-shrine,
And from the heavens and earth which, hitherto,
Were with the glory of His presence filled.
And now as one who gropes in starless night,
And blindly stumbles on familiar paths,
Growing half doubtful of realities
Trusted, without a question, in the light,
Believing half in thronging fantasies
That haunt his mind bewildered—so it was,
In ever growing measure, with the king.

Then, as the dreadful void grew absolute,
And as the midnight darkness more and more
Inwrapped him, and his last faint, wavering prayer
Of dying faith, unheeded or unanswered,
Sank into stifling depths of voiceless gloom,
There came to him those questionings of himself,

And of all things, yea, even of the One
From whom are all things, who is over all,
That spring inevitably from such a state
Of spiritual night and loneliness,
In soul so great as that of Solomon.

As with a fevered brain, in broken dreams,
Wearied, but resting not, he vainly strove
To pierce the mysteries of life and death;
And grappled ceaselessly with problems vast,
And ever burdened with the bootless quest
After the fathomless cause and origin
Of evil in the universe of God,
Or final goal and issue unrevealed
Whereto its unarrested progress tends;
Or miseries great and multitudinous
Of human life—the heart's deep bitterness,
Wrongs unavenged, strange inequalities,
And seeming emptiness and vanity
Of man's endeavors, even of his gains,
His triumphs and his joys, when comes the end
Alike to him who smiles and him who weeps.

And so, with God thus dimly far removed,

Or veiled in frowning clouds impervious,
And hence His wisdom, righteousness and love—
The explanations ample, infinite
Of all that else bewilders human minds
Or tortures doubting hearts—no longer now
Believed in, realized, as in the past,
The last, worst stage of his apostacy
Had come to Solomon. In dark despair,
Most of himself but much of all beside
That once had been the anchors of his soul,
He drifted out upon a stormy sea.
And not as ofttimes fleetly rides unharmed
The light unladen barque, like bubble tossed
Upon the crested wave. Oh, rather he
Was as the huge leviathan of the deep,
The ocean ship of towering masts, and sails
Wide spread to all the winds, and freighted full,
Which, with the shattering force its might insures,
Strikes, tempest-driven, on the hidden rocks,
And through its greatness greater ruin finds.
Alas, thus forcefully, disastrously,
This one whom God had dowered with kingly gifts,
And matchless largeness of a generous heart,
Having thus madly thrust away the conscience

That once had held him to the truth and right,
Made shipwreck of his faith and of himself.

For God, his father's God, was, at the most,
Only to him a vague abstraction now ;
And scarce more in his feeling and his life
Than if He were not.  And it seemed to him
As if the man had no pre-eminence,
In nature, dignity or destiny,
Above the dumbly grazing animal ;
That both were but the victims or the sport
Of fate or time and chance, whose happenings
Unguided came impartially to all ;
And that to eat and drink with merry heart,
Forgetting as he might his hastening end,
Was after all the highest good for man.

Such atrophy of feeling and of faith
Brought speedy consequent paralysis
To all that once were reigning faculties
Within the lofty soul of Solomon.
The checks that lingering wisdom exercised
Upon his errant senses, restive grown,
Were ineffective now as silken threads

In palsied hands, on necks of tameless steeds.
Hence, urged by cravings ever unappeased,
And ever more insatiable the more
The husks of sense were vainly fed upon,
He plunged with reckless self-abandonment
Into excesses, ruinous as well
To outraged body as polluted soul.
Mad dissipations, gross indulgences
Wrought the corroding and enfeebling work
Of age upon him, blanched his raven hair
And dimmed the brightness of his eagle glance,
Clouded his once serene and regal brow,
And robbed his mind and frame of energy,
Ere scarce had come to him the autumn-time
That else had only brought his ripened powers
To full development and crowning grace.

Thus apathetic and indifferent
To what was true or false or right or wrong,
His very manhood broken and disrobed
Of all but mocking show of royalty,
He reached, with tottering steps, the farthest stage
Of his wild wandering—crime and infamy.

The once fair Naamah, now long misnamed,
Had noted, with keen-sighted jealousy,
The exclusive favor manifestly shown
To her Egyptian rival. She alone,
Of all the wives of Solomon, was free
To cherish and to worship openly
Her country's gods. Under the shadowing groves
Around her palace gleamed the images
Of Isis and Osiris, on whose altars
Her votive offerings were duly laid.
But Naamah as yet had vainly plead
Like coveted privilege for herself and for
The Ammonitish women in her train.
Now, in her cultured cunning (crowning trait
Of feminine intellect in harems trained),
She saw and seized her opportunity;
And common cause she made with other wives
Of heathen nations,—Hittites, Moabites,
Sidonians, Tyrians—and she artfully
Fomented in their breasts the wide-spread leaven
Of envious discontent, till, even beyond
The harem's walls, their fellow countrymen
Who thronged Jerusalem had ere long caught
The stealthily wafted spirit of unrest,

And swelled the clamor, now no more repressed,
For equal and impartial liberty,
To each and all, of worshiping the gods
Their nations served, or such as pleased them best.

Worn with excesses, prematurely old,
Infirm of will, unfortified by faith,
Wearied with ceaseless importunities,
Most by his wives' caresses weakly won,
The craven king succumbed, and presently
Upon the summit of the hill that fronts
Jehovah's temple, on Moriah throned,
Were reared the altars of their heathen gods.
Around them fast they flock exultingly,
And in the sight of grieving worshipers
Of Him who is the only living God,
The smoke of incense and of sacrifice
Gathers like frowning clouds upon the sky.

Oh, tell it not in Gath, publish it not
In streets of Askelon, that he who lies,
Self-ruined, prostrate in this depth of shame,
Is Israel's king, beloved of Israel's God,
Honored and crowned with wisdom's starry crown,
Thus tarnished and of majesty despoiled!

For now on Judah's soil, by his command,
In insolent defiance, on the heights
That overlook Jerusalem, behold,
Moab's abomination, Chemosh stood,
And loathèd Milcom of the Ammonites—
By others Molech named—grim, hideous,
With brazen hands outstretched for shrinking babes,
That on them turned to ashes in the blaze
Of the fierce furnace which beneath them burned.
(This only in his native lands; as yet
Such horror was unwrought in Israel.)
Nor distant far Sidonian Ashteroth,
Star-goddess, otherwise as Venus known
Or Aphrodite born of the sea-foam,
The fabled queen of beauty and of love;
Worshiped with rites that oft were foully stained,
And cruelly, with mingled lust and blood.

At first the recreant monarch did no more
Than yield his royal sanction, listlessly,
To that which all his sluggish feeling held
Repulsive or as only food for scorn;
But as, from day to day, within his sight
These heathen altars blazed, and round them stood

Or bowed, or whirled in frantic heathen dance,
Not foreigners alone or but his wives
And concubines, but also Israelites—
So strangely prone to leave their purer shrines
For soul-besotting idol vanities,—
As at a distance thus the king looked on,
There subtly stole upon him more and more
The fatal fascination which inheres
In every scene of evil so beheld,
Without the counteraction or restraint
That steadfast loyalty, to sacred right
And God, alone assures. Nor was it long
Before his erring feet had carried him
Where first his yielding heart had led the way.

Awhile it seemed that, at this nearer view
Of rites idolatrous, abominable,
His soul the more recoiled. Relentlessly
He poured contempt upon them all, nor less
Upon himself, his weakness and his folly
To which the wanton insult, by them cast
On Israel and Israel's God, was due.
Nor ever, in the future, came to him
Aught but a dulling sense of what was true,

Or deepening disregard of what was right.
And so, in utmost climax of his guilt
And impious presumption, recklessly,
Knowing but heeding not the wrong he did,
At last, beside his wives he bowed the head
With holy oil anointed, kissed the hand
Before Jehovah's altars oft upraised,
And, with such forms of reverence unfelt,
Did homage to the gods of wood and stone !

Once, but once only.   On that dreadful day,
Which proved a very midnight to his soul,
His long beclouded intellect grew clear,
And all its torpid, weakened faculties
Were fitfully stirred to unaccustomed strength.
Scarcely had passed the impulse unforeseen,
And all inexplicable to his thought,
That made him what alike he cursed and scorned,
A thrall of shrewish wives ! idolater !
When instantly, as by the lightning's flash
That rives the darkness, making brightly bare
Whate'er was covered by its pall of gloom,
There stood revealed to his adjudging self
What now he was, and what he once had been,

And all the windings of the downward way,
That stretched afar between the bliss-fraught past
And present degradation and despair.

The night that closed upon that day of shame
Brought no oblivious sleep to Solomon :
But from its depths emerged, ere morning came,
The image that had faded from his mind,
And from his dreams had vanished long ago,—
The face of Sulamith, so sadly sweet,
Still half averted, distant, shadow-like,
Wearing that last inexorable look,
Which yet, with love and grief unspeakable,
Softened the pain with which it wrung his heart ;
With eyes of melting pity or reproach,
Or shrinking as from something loathed and feared ;
But more, with wooing, winning tenderness,
Such as a grieving angel's face might wear,
When pleading, angel-like, with one he watched
And warded, who had strayed in evil ways.

When gloomily dawned at length the tardy
    morn,
The crashing thunders of a tempest shook

The palace walls.  Then, to the awe-struck king,
There came a voice, above the tempest's roar,
Though uttered softly as a breeze's sigh,
Or, as the murmur of a meadow brook ;
Twice heard in by-gone years, its thrilling tones
Unchanged, but ah, how sternly different
Its fateful import now !—Jehovah's voice,
Which to the already self-condemning king
His accusation and his sentence spoke :

"Forasmuch, as this, of which thou knowest,
Is done of thee, and my covenants and
Statutes, which I commanded thee, thou hast
Not kept, thy kingdom from thee shall be rent,
And to thy servant given.  Yet in thy days
This shall not be, for David, thy father's sake ;
But from thy son's hands I will rend the kingdom.
Howbeit, not all ; but one tribe I will give him,
For David's sake and for Jerusalem's."

The storm's commotion and the "still small
          voice"
Together into solemn silence died.
Then Solomon arose and went his way,

As one who knew or partly knew his doom,
And hoped no more,—submissive, resolute
To meet the worst and bear it patiently.
The glowing wine cup on his laden board
He left unquaffed, and of the dainty meats
He tasted not; and all that day he gave
To much neglected business of his realm.
With wisdom worthy of his better years,
And energy unmatched in all the past,
He laid his plans and issued his commands
For rapid and effectual quieting
Of popular unrest; for crushing out
Beginnings of revolt in vassal-lands,
And for the overthrow of idol-worship
From Dan even unto Beer-sheba.
And sternly he decreed that whosoe'er—
Whether a stranger or an Israelite,
Or of the very household of the king—
Thenceforth bowed down to graven images,
Should suffer instant banishment, or if
Still lingering found should without pity die.

Another day of abstinence and toil,
Then to his trusted councilors the king

Made full committal of the kingdom's rule,
While he should seek the rest and quietness
His shaken health required.  With but his guards
And necessary servants, he repaired
With urgent speed to Lebanon's retreats ;
And in the summer-palace, beautiful
With pillared porches, all of cedar wrought,
He found the solitude for which he longed.
All royal state he steadfastly abjured ;
Uncrowned was now his bowed and hoary head,
And plainly robed his still majestic form :
And they who watched him closely, anxiously,
Troubled for both his reason and his life,
Noted how seldom and how sparingly
He ever ate of even the simplest food ;
But most of all they grieved to see him lie
Day after day upon his chamber floor,
In sackcloth clothed, with shrouded face and still,
As if already numbered with the dead.

A change passed over him.  His eye again
With something of its wonted brightness beamed,
And on his pallid cheek would glow and fade
The flush that once had lingered fadeless there.

An impulse from within and from above
Now moved upon him, as the waking winds
Upon a ship becalmed on stagnant seas.
His pen and parchment—lately little used—
For long, swift hours he plies, all else unheeded;
And lo, a record of his inner life
Flows from his guided hand, resembling much
Its broken current and its waywardness;
Its turbulent revolt against the bounds
That would have kept it in a tranquil course,
Unruffled, widening, deepening to its goal;
Its surging doubts, its black and sunless pools
Of unbelief; its chafing on the rocks
Of truth and right, eternity and God;
Its final turning to the only way
That wins at last the shoreless, welcoming sea,
To be in it forever lost and found—
The way of reverence and obedience,
The fear of God and His commandments kept,—
The crowning good of life, the whole of man!

And now the angel who hath power of dreams,
And at whose wavèd wand illusion seems
More brightly real than the common things
That wakeful sense to wakeful mind oft brings,
As though his task were ended, spread his wings;
And only to the wistful dreamer's prayer
His flight awhile consented to forbear;
And then the eyelids lightly sealed in sleep
He gently touched, and made the slumber deep,
A trancèd spell, in which the spirit's eye
Could more than scenes and shapes and acts descry,—
Could even look upon the world of thought,
The soul's ideals ere to being brought,
The very concepts, else unseen, unheard,
Waiting their birth-time through the living word;
And—as from far above—a golden beam
Flashed and illumed the mystery of the dream.

## XVI.

## THE SONG OF SONGS.

**A**NOTHER change passed over Solomon.
   It was as when, on cedared Lebanon,
   The soft south winds of early spring-time
      blow,
And turn to gushing streams the wintry snow,
Until its slopes—first bared, then clothed with green—
How .soon enwreathed with clustering flowers are
   seen !
And so to his long sad and frozen heart
A spring-like breath did melting warmth impart ;
And tender feelings waked that long had slept;
The fount of tears was stirred, the monarch wept.
No more his broken, ineffectual prayer
Seemed dead, lost words upon the heedless air,
But, from the now no longer far-off Heaven,
The whispered answer came, " Thou art forgiven."
So from him passed the wintry death and gloom,

And delicate flowers of peace had sudden bloom.
As in his soul with growing brightness beamed
The dawn-light, which at first so faintly gleamed,—
Still chastened, penitent,—he felt and seemed
As one from whom has slipped away at last
That worn, stained garment, his polluted past,
And who, now purged from all its filthiness,
Puts on the pure, white robe of holiness.

When thus the wasted years for Solomon—
His years of guilt and shame—had dream-like gone,
The spring-time of his life came back anew,
Its balmy air and skies of cloudless blue,
Its blending melodies of brook and breeze,
And bird-notes trilling from the leafy trees,
And—welcomed most of the returning train—
He sees unchanged his youth's sole love again.
He hears, with raptured heart and charmèd ear,
The whispers low which tell that she is near,
And notes with olden bliss her blushes rise,
While gazing long into her deep dark eyes.
Oh, much is his of all for which he longs,
Rays of her brightness, snatches of her songs.
As oft before, still side by side they stand

On rocky heights by mountain breezes fanned,
And see far cities and the silvery gleam,
On distant plain, of interlacing stream;
Or far below, beneath the vine-roofed bowers,
Their fond communings wing the happy hours.

But more immeasurably than memories fraught
With all the bliss that earthly love ere brought,
Held in his heart of hearts above them far
As above hearth-fire shines a quenchless star,
Was that pure passion thus o'er-mastering grown,
Exalted to his soul's supremest throne—
His love for God, his life, a breath of Heaven—
Much did he love, for much was he forgiven!
Yet from the earth-born love that freshly burns,
And purely in his chastened heart, he learns,
With quickened sense and spirit-guided thought,
Full many a lesson else perchance untaught;
And from the lower, as on stairs of gold,
Mounts to the higher, to the things untold,
Which hearts conceive not, nor do eyes behold.

Now to the king, absorbed in love and praise
And ceaseless holy joys, swift sped the days

Until they brought a still and starless night,
In which the voice thrice heard commanded "write!"
And, with the theme that filled his soul supplied,
He wrote, but not without an unseen guide.


As one of subtile sense and open ears
To catch, enrapt, the music of the spheres,
And dowered with art, through more than royal
    birth,
To wake the answering harmonies of earth,—
As such a crownèd king of melody
Might cull fit sounds for tuneful rhapsody :
The dulcet notes that tell the heart's delight,
The weird and thrilling voices of the night,
The choral warblings of the happy birds,
The softened lowings of the distant herds,
The rain drops pattering and the plash of oar,
The brooklet's lulling song, the cataract's roar,
The fitful wind's Eolian minstrelsy,
The murmurs deep of never resting sea,
The peals of bells and laughter ringing high,
And roll of thunder-drums along the sky—
Might from the various sounds of nature choose
Such as were meet, and all beside refuse ;

Even so did Israel's reanointed king,
Heaven-taught, from all his treasured memories
    bring
Such as were worthy, and from these he wove
His mystic song of longing and of love.

    Sweet oriental idyll of the heart!
Artless creation of consummate art ;
Its sources, nature, life, reality,
But from their limitations strangely free ;
Wrought of the ever marred, imperfect real
Into the unmarred, perfected ideal—
The type in Eden lost, blent sanctity
And blessedness of wedded unity ;
Picture of simple joys and beauties fraught
With meanings that transcend all earth-bound
    thought ;
A pastoral poem, and yet a prophecy
Of love's great King and kingdom that should be,
And day of His espousals which imparts
Its everlasting joy to yearning hearts.

    Whoso this Song of Songs would read aright
Must read with single eye, with purgèd sight,

14

Else on its fair, chaste lines he may but see
The shadows of his own impurity.
Who purely reads, though but from nature's plane,
Much of delight and profit yet may gain;
May feast his mind and soul on beauties rare,
Scale mountain heights and breathe their freshened
    air,
Acquire for noble uses deepened sense
Of heart-worth—love and truth and innocence—
A priceless boon! But tenfold happier he,
Who from the bondage of the letter free,
And spirit-led and lighted, finds the key
That opes its shrined and sacred mystery.

Fast from the flying pen of Solomon
The stream of song had flowed. His task was done.
As twilight shadows softly round him crept,
Exhausted with his pleasing toil, he slept;
And motionless upon his couch he lay
Till came the wakening light of new-born day.

Over his face its kindling radiance streamed ;
He smiled, as if a happy dream he dreamed.
Still through the casement flowed the waves of gold —
Ah! changeless smile, on lips so pale and cold.
The river rests, since it has reached the sea ;
Life's turbulence ends in death's tranquillity.
How royally, when baffled strivings cease,
The lofty brow is crowned with holy peace !

THE END.

# NOTE.

CAREFUL Bible readers, who may have deigned
to favor this volume with their attention, may not
unwarrantably criticise its representation of Solomon's exclusive devotion to Sulamith, at the beginning of his reign of forty years, previous to his
affinity with Naamah, the mother of Rehoboam
who, after Solomon's death, ascended the throne at
the age of forty-one years.

It can only be said in deprecation of such anticipated criticism, First, that romance writers are not
to be held to strict historical accuracy; and, Second,
that the seeming anachronism may be relieved by
the consideration that the length of the lives and
the reigns of David, Solomon, Rehoboam and, gen-
erally, their successors, are only given in round
numbers; and further, that the beginning of Rehoboam's reign may have been fixed, by its chroni-
cler, at the date of the convocation of the tribes,
when he was formally invested with the kingdom,
at Shechem, which would seem to have taken place
more than a year after the death of Solomon. See
"Hours with the Bible," vol. iv. page 2.